Mr. Darcy's Angel of Mercy

Mary Lydon Simonsen

Quail Creek Publishing, LLC
http://marysimonsenfanfiction.blogspot.com
http://www.austenauthors.net

Printed in the United States of America

quailcreekpub@hotmail.com
www.marysimonsenfanfiction.blogspot.com

©2011 Quail Creek Publishing LLC
Peoria, Arizona

ISBN-10: 0615475671
ISBN-13: 978-0615475677

Mr. Darcy's Angel of Mercy

A Pride and Prejudice Re-Imagining

Prologue

Front Line, France
June 1918

"Sir, if I may speak," Sergeant Mercer asked.

"No, you may not. You are neither my mother nor my physician. You are my batman. Is that clear?" Captain Darcy asked as he coughed out the words. He knew he was sick and that he should go to the infirmary, but he was not about to abandon his men two days before a big push was scheduled. *An officer leads from the front.* That basic military tenet had been drilled into his head during officer training, and he would not deviate from it. He waved his aide off, turning his attention to the orders he had received from headquarters.

"Sir," Mercer said, catapulting out of his seat. Darcy, who believed he was about to be subjected to another lecture about his health, was prepared to give his batman a dressing down that he would never forget when he followed Mercer's eyes and found them glued to the figure of Colonel Bradford, or Bloody Bradford, as he was known by his troops. He, too, led from the front and had the battle scars to prove it.

Darcy jumped to attention. But the sudden movement caused him to break out into a fit of coughing, and he was unable to properly acknowledge his superior officer.

"So the reports I have been hearing that you are seriously ill are accurate," the colonel said when Darcy was finally able to control his hacking. "You are hereby ordered to report to the infirmary at once."

"Sir, there is a big push scheduled for the 17th."

"*You* are telling *me* that there is push on for the 17th? It was I who planned the whole bloody thing for our sector. But if you think that I am going to allow one of my junior officers to lead a company of men into battle when he is obviously unfit for service…"

"Sir…"

"Don't you dare interrupt me, Captain. You may think you are indispensible to winning this damned war, but HQ thinks otherwise. Lieutenant Tetley has been assigned to take over your company."

"Permission to speak, sir." After the colonel

nodded his assent, Darcy continued. "My men and I have formed a cohesive unit, and they will follow…"

"They will follow whomever I tell them to follow," the colonel bellowed, but soon lowered his voice. Darcy was a damn fine officer, who had been mentioned several times in dispatches. There was no one better to take his company over the top. But only if he was fit for duty, and he wasn't. "Now, believe it or not, I have more important things to do than to go up and down the line to see if my officers are exercising proper judgment. You will report to the infirmary, and I shall not hear another word about it."

"Yes, sir," Darcy answered, throwing his shoulders back.

As soon as Colonel Bradford left, Darcy collapsed on his camp bed, wiping his fevered brow with his handkerchief.

"Good Lord, Mercer. What am I to do? Lieutenant Tetley is fresh off the boat from England with no mud on his boots, and the men are expected to follow him into battle?"

"Sir, you're seriously ill," his batman said. "And remember, you were once wet behind the ears just like Lieutenant Tetley. Every officer has to experience his first battle, and so it will be for the lieutenant."

"But this isn't some six-man patrol going out to mend the wire or to round up a few prisoners. This is a major push to recover the ground we gave up in April."

"Sir, you would be disobeying a direct order if you do not report to the infirmary," Mercer said, reminding his young officer of what Colonel Bradford had said.

Darcy lowered his shoulders in resignation. "Get Sergeant Major Sullivan in here for a briefing. He is Tetley's only hope of surviving the push."

But that was Darcy's last order to his batman. By the time, his sergeant had returned with Sullivan, the young captain was experiencing delirium associated with a high fever, and Sullivan and Mercer would man both ends of the stretcher taking the captain to the infirmary nestled in an apple orchard behind the reserve lines. From there, he would be transferred to the hospital at Le Touquet where a steady stream of suspected influenza cases was already lining the halls of the former casino.

* * *

Le Touquet Hospital

"Elizabeth, Sister wants to see you."

Lizzy looked at her fellow VAD for some

indication of what she had done wrong this time, but Catherine merely shrugged her shoulders. When she had signed up to become a Voluntary Aid Detachment, Lizzy had been told that she would receive hands-on training as a nurse's aide and would learn from her mistakes. But she was beginning to think that learning from her mistakes was the only way she learned anything. As hard as she tried, Sister McCrory always found fault with her work, but according to Sister, she must make no complaint. "After all, you are here to make life better for the patients, not the other way 'round."

"Miss Bennet, please sit down," Sister McCrory said. Since Sister never allowed any VAD to be seated in her presence, Lizzy knew that bad news was coming, and she wondered if she was being sent back to the ships that took the wounded to England, or worse, an ignominious return home because her supervisor had determined that her young charge was unequal to the task of caring for gravely wounded men. With her mind creating every possible scenario for her dismissal, Lizzy reluctantly sat on the wooden chair in front of Sister's desk.

"Do you know Lieutenant Jeremy Lucas?" Sister asked.

"Yes, Sister, we have been friends since we were children in Hertfordshire."

"I have received word that Lieutenant Lucas has been wounded and is in Ward 18 and has asked that you visit him."

Lizzy had been corresponding with Jeremy ever since her friend and neighbor had joined the British Expeditionary Force in August 1916. Since so many men were needed to fill the ranks following the bloodbath on the Somme, a battle that had killed 20,000 British soldiers on the first day, the nineteen-year old had left the University of Sheffield and enlisted in the king's army. Because of their exchange of letters, Jeremy knew that Elizabeth was working at the base hospital in Le Touquet.

The hospital had been set up in 1914 during the early days of the war by the Duchess of Westminster in a casino situated in a beautiful forest at a time when people actually believed that the "the show" would be over by Christmas. Chandeliers that had once shined their enchanted light on men in black tie and tails and women accoutered in gorgeous evening gowns and jewels were now draped with linen covers, and its gaming tables, where fortunes had been won and lost, had been removed to make way for hospital beds. The final evidence of its former glory had been erased when the private salons had been converted into operating theaters, and the parquet floors, formerly trod by the elite of Europe, were now stained with the blood of the youth of France and Britain.

"Visit Lieutenant Lucas? Do you mean after I am off duty?" Surely, she did not mean that she should leave in the middle of her rotation. Sister would never allow such a thing.

"No, Elizabeth, I do not want you to wait. You need to go now."

Did Sister just call me Elizabeth? And with that familiar term of address, all confusion disappeared. The only reason she had been called into her office was because Jeremy Lucas was dying.

Lizzy remained frozen in place, staring at her hands, and shaking her head in denial that yet another of her friends was about to leave her. The list had grown so long: John Lucas, Matthew Gardiner, Robert Long, Adam Hill, and on and on *ad nauseum.*

"Elizabeth, Lieutenant Lucas has a stomach wound, and he is not responding to treatment. Ward 18. Go now," she said, pointing in the direction of the temporary wards that had been set up following the launch of the German's spring offensive.

Because of the ferocity of the offensive, the hospitals that had been established after the Battles of Ypres and the Somme and that now dotted the Atlantic coast from Ostend in Belgium to Cherbourg in Normandy were full once again. Although the enemy had been checked, the fighting continued on into April, May, and now June, and even the four hundred hospital beds of the casino proved to be inadequate. Tent wards built on wooden platforms or buildings made of wood that could be erected in one day had sprung up to handle the steady flow of sick and wounded, and in one of those interim structures, Jeremy Lucas awaited his friend.

Lizzy raced toward Ward 18, and when she arrived, she found its entrance blocked by ambulances that had backed up to its double doors. The hospital wagons would take the wounded to the port of Boulogne, the first leg of their journey to England. From there, the soldiers would be segregated based on the severity of their wounds. The walking wounded would watch as endless stretchers, bearing their more seriously wounded comrades, were carried on to the hospital ships waiting in the harbor. Once in Blighty, they would be placed on hospital trains that would travel to the farthest reaches of England and Scotland to take the wounded to hospitals closest to their homes and families. With the VADs busily engaged in supervising the orderlies for the loading of the patients, Lizzy went unobserved into the ward and soon found Jeremy.

"Lizzy, you have come," Jeremy said, reaching

out to touch Elizabeth. "I had no idea if my message got through."

"Yes, I have come," Lizzy said, taking his hand.

"Your beautiful curls are all covered up," Jeremy whispered, and Lizzy reached up and pulled her head covering off and shook her head liberating her untamed tresses. "Much better," he said, admiring his beautiful childhood friend. "You are out of breath. Did you run? I imagine you did. Just like when we used to play football on the village green. You shamed all the boys."

Lizzy soaked a cloth in water and placed it on Jeremy's brow, and when an orderly approached asking if he should get one of the nurses, Lizzy shook her head. After sixteen months as a VAD, she recognized the sights and smells of death. There was nothing to be gained by taking others away from their duties.

"I always thought you should have been a boy, but thank God you weren't or you would have been in this meat grinder with John and me. Have you had any news about John?"

Lizzy shook her head. No, she had heard nothing, nor would she. John had been killed in Italy the previous year.

"No news is good news or that's what they keep

telling me."

"I *have* had a letter from Charlotte," Lizzy said, trying desperately to retain her composure and a steadiness in her voice. "She has completed her nurse's training at London General Hospital, and we must all address her as 'Sister' now. She quite outranks us."

"Charlotte? Who is Charlotte? Oh, yes, I remember. Dear old Charlotte." Then Jeremy clutched her hand so tightly, as hundreds before him had done, and the words he spoke no longer made any sense, and Lizzy held his hand until there was a stillness and a final breath, and Jeremy Lucas, twenty-two years of age, was no more.

Lizzy had no idea how long she had been sitting there when she felt the orderly's hand on her shoulder. "We have to take him now, miss," he said, cupping his ear as a way to cue her to the muffled sound of the guns in the distance. "We're going to need the bed."

Clutching her head covering, Lizzy walked to the rear of the ward. She had nearly reached the exit when she heard the faint cry of "nurse."

Oh, please, no. I don't want to do anything for anyone tonight. But then Lizzy heard the voice again asking for "water," and she knew she must respond.

The patient, surrounded by screens, had been segregated from the others, and she quickly glanced at his chart to find the cause for his isolation. "Under observation - possible influenza" was written across the bottom. She deliberately avoided looking at the name on the chart. In that way, if he died, she wouldn't recognize his name when it appeared on the casualty lists. She placed her hand on his forehead and found that he had a low-grade fever, and after putting her head on his chest, she listened for indications of pneumonia. Before she could lift her head, the officer had placed his hand on her hair and ran his fingers down the side of her face, and she feared that she would collapse into a pool of tears at the gentleness of his gesture.

Satisfied that his condition did not preclude his having water, she propped him up so that he might drink from the glass, and when he asked her what her name was, she shook her head. "No names. Just think of me as a visiting angel. Please just sip the water," she cautioned him. He did as she asked.

"Will you stay for a few minutes, my angel of mercy? You don't have to say anything. If you would just hold my hand, it would be enough."

Lizzy placed a chair next to his bed and took the officer's hand. But then she reached into her pocket and retrieved a handkerchief. "Sorry. I am a bit weepy this evening."

"I understand. You lost a patient tonight." Lizzy looked at him with a puzzled expression. "The orderlies and aides are very methodical about their duties, but after four days, one comes to recognize the sounds that follow the death of a patient. Everyone tries to be quiet, but it is not possible to make no noise at all."

Lizzy listened to the sound of his soothing voice and was comforted by it, and then he covered her hand with his and caressed it with his thumb. After looking into her eyes, he pulled her towards him until she was sitting beside him on the bed. When she felt his lips on hers, at first all she could think about was that this would be her last day as a VAD and that she would be sent home in disgrace, but she soon found that she did not care. She responded to his searching mouth and his every touch, and without really thinking about what she was doing, she placed her head covering on the chair, took off her shoes, and after removing her white apron, she got into bed with the patient and lay next to him.

Lizzy was awakened by the sound of the VADs making their rounds, and after one glance at the sleeping officer, she picked up her discarded clothing and went quickly out the back door into a moonless night.

Chapter 1

"Darcy, I didn't think you would ever get here," Charles Bingley said, shaking his friend's hand as his visitor emerged from his automobile.

"I think the whole of Hertfordshire is under construction," Darcy said, while removing his driving cap and traveling coat. "They are working on the road south of Watford, and I had to take a detour. It had me going so far east that I thought I would end up taking in a view of the North Sea."

"Why didn't you take the train? I could have picked you up at the station and saved you the bother. But I know the answer to that question. You wanted to show off the Silver Ghost," Bingley said as he walked around Darcy's 1913 Rolls Royce. "I can hardly believe your cousin sold it to you."

"It helps that Antony is desperately in need of cash," Darcy said. "I got it for a song."

Darcy had been after his cousin, Antony, Lord Stepton, to sell him the Ghost since Darcy had got out of hospital a year earlier. When it came down to either selling the Rolls Royce or the lease on his townhouse, Antony, who always wanted to be in the thick of things in town as well as being the center of attention, would not sell the lease.

After giving the Rolls Royce the attention it deserved, Bingley asked his friend what he thought of the manor house. Before answering, Darcy climbed up the first step of the porch and felt a piece of concrete start to give way.

"Watch out, Darcy. It's a little tricky there," Bingley cautioned his friend.

"Blast it, Bingley, this whole slab is falling apart," and Darcy kicked at another piece of buckling concrete.

"Yes, I know," Bingley said with a nervous laugh. "Remember the ice storm that hit the South Midlands last winter? Well, it did a lot of damage to Netherfield Park as well."

The purpose of Darcy's visit was to have a good look at the manor house that Bingley had rented for the coming year. As part of his inspection, Darcy walked down the drive so that he might have the benefit of the long view. What he saw was a Georgian manor house in a state of decay. The columns on the portico were cracked, the window frames were rotted, and what stucco remained in place was chipped or peeling, exposing the red brick beneath. The whole thing desperately needed a coat of paint and that was just the house.

After making inquiries in town, Darcy had learned that at one time Netherfield Park could boast of some of the finest gardens in Hertfordshire. But as he walked the gardens, there was little evidence of its former glory. The grounds had been neglected to the point that it was more of a wildness area than anything else.

"Charles, this house is in a serious state of disrepair," Darcy said while looking at the rear façade that was in worse condition than the front of the house. "For God sakes, you can't even walk out your back door without putting your life in peril. Why ever did you sign a lease on such a wreck of a place?"

"Oh, I didn't sign a lease. I bought it outright. The Darlingtons wanted to move to Canada, and they needed to settle quickly. I obliged. It was an absolute steal."

"It was a steal? May I ask who was stealing from whom?" Darcy said as he surveyed the knee-deep grass, shapeless hedges, idle fountain, and heaving stones on the paths and patio. "Charles, I know you have piles of money stacked up in a bank in Birmingham, but even so…"

"Oh, come on, Darce, think of the advantages: easy access to London by car or train, clean country air, a dance hall, and sprightly country lasses in need of dance partners."

Darcy burst out laughing. "The whole bloody country is teeming with sprightly lasses in need of partners. There must be twenty women for every man with two legs left to him."

"Well, we will find out soon enough as there is a dance in Meryton this Saturday."

"Not for me, Old Boy," Darcy said, shaking his head. "I have been to a few of these country dances, and as soon as you walk in the door, every pair of female eyes locks in on you. It's like a stag hunt, and we are the prey."

"Listen, Darcy. I need to do this. I think I have finally got the hang of this artificial foot, and I want to test it out. Here in the country, the ladies don't care if a man makes a misstep or two. They are just happy to see a man under the age of forty paying them a bit of attention."

Darcy knew how his friend had struggled in his quest to find a prosthetic device that fit properly, and the awkwardness of his gait had sapped some of

Bingley's gushing enthusiasm for just about everything. Even so, Darcy was surprised by his friend's reticence. He was handsome, very rich, and available, and of the three, it was the last that counted the most. With a generation of men lost in the trenches of the Western Front, even some of the titled ladies in London had indicated that despite his being the son of an industrial titan they would welcome his advances. After studying his friend, he realized that Bingley really *did* need to do this. Since it didn't seem like a lot to ask, Darcy finally agreed.

"I will go, but on one condition. You allow me to find my own dance partners. I don't want you steering any girls in my direction. I don't need any help in that regard."

Bingley slapped his friend on the back before gesturing for Darcy to go into the house ahead of him.

"No thanks. You go first. You know where it is safe to walk." And Darcy followed in Charles's carefully placed footsteps.

Chapter 2

"Netherfield is *not* let," Mrs. Bennet said as her family gathered for lunch following Sunday services.

"Francine, did you not tell us all last night that Netherfield Park *was* let?" Thomas Bennet asked his wife.

"I did. But after church today, I learned from Mrs. Long that the Darlingtons have *sold* the property, not rented it. Apparently, they have gone to live in Canada." She then made a face to indicate her disapproval of their decision.

In Mrs. Bennet's mind, the Dominion of Canada and the United States contained vast swaths of land peopled by red men and cowboys, all of whom carried guns or axes for felling trees, and although she sang *Rule Britannia* as loudly as the next Englishman, she was uneasy about some of the consequences of having an empire spanning the globe. After seeing men of a dozen nations walking the streets of London during the war, including some "who wore turbans and were very dark," Mrs. Bennet's natural xenophobia had become more pronounced, especially when a few of the Hottentots dared to venture into the countryside on picnics or to view some of the local sites.

"The Darlingtons have lived at Netherfield Park since George III sat on the throne." Mrs. Bennet did not understand why any Englishman would want to live anywhere other than on "this blessed plot, this earth, this realm, this England."

"Because their daughter and grandson live in Toronto," Jane explained to her mother, "and Lucy is their only surviving child, it makes sense for them to go where their family is."

"Will Sir Arthur remain a knight?"

"Yes, of course," Jane answered. "Canada *is* in the Commonwealth, and they are not relinquishing their British citizenship."

"I believe we were speaking of Charles Bingley," Mr. Bennet said, tapping the table with his finger. "From what I have read in the financials in *The Times*, I can tell you that he is the heir to the Bingley Iron Works in Birmingham. How rich is Mr. Bingley, you may ask, my dear? I shall tell you that the Aga Khan is nothing to him."

"Oh my! That is very rich indeed," Mrs. Bennet said, nodding her head in approval.

"I know something about the family as well," Kitty said. The twenty-one-year-old was a voracious consumer of magazines that featured stories about the lives of film stars, ingénues, society's elite and the fashions they wore. "Charles Bingley and his sister, Caroline, are frequently mentioned in *The Tatler*. I have seen photographs of both, and they are very attractive. But I think something happened to Mr. Bingley during the war."

"Kitty, that statement is true for ninety percent of Englishmen," Lizzy said, while continuing to read the Sunday paper.

"Please tell us what you know," a curious Jane asked. The eldest Bennet daughter, who was nearing her twenty-eighth birthday, was thrilled to think that a single man was practically living next door to them. She did not care how rich he was. All she wanted to know was did the man dance.

"I know that his sister, Louisa, is married to Edward Hurst, who was arrested for drunkenness in Piccadilly Square. When the policeman was taking him into custody, Mr. Hurst asked, 'Do you know who I am? I am Edward Hurst, and my brother is a director for Inland Revenue,' and the bobby said that he wouldn't hold that against him. Isn't that funny?

And his sister Caroline, who runs with the Sloane Square crowd, is always wearing the latest fashions from Paris. She has broken two engagements, and now *The Tatler* is saying that she has set her sights on a certain Fitzwilliam Darcy who is Mr. Bingley's closest associate."

"And who is this Mr. Darcy?" her mother asked Kitty. "Is he equally rich?"

"It seems that the gentleman's ancestors were Normans who came over with William the Conqueror, and one of them was in the field at Runnymede when King John signed the Magna Carter. At least that is what *Inside London* is reporting. His father is Sir David Darcy, and his mother is Lady Anne, the daughter of the late Earl of Stepton."

Lizzy was amused at Kitty's capacity to store so much information in her brain about complete strangers but could not name all the counties bordering Hertfordshire. If only high society and the cinema had been a part of the curriculum, she would have performed better in school.

"But is Mr. Darcy rich?" Mrs. Bennet asked, continuing to press.

"The article said that the Darcys own a vast estate somewhere in the north Midlands, so I imagine that they are rich."

"If I remember correctly, Sir David Darcy served in Lloyd George's government as a liaison with Naval Intelligence," Mr. Bennet said. "It is my understanding that the weight of his duties brought on a nervous breakdown, and after the war, he and his wife moved to the South of France for some peace and quiet."

Mr. Bennet also knew of reports published after the war that indicated German U-boats had sunk more than one-half million tons of British shipping, a figure kept from the people of Britain for fear that it would weaken their will to fight on. As far as Mr. Bennet was concerned, Sir David was entitled to his breakdown.

"Well, let us hope that he is nothing like his cousin, the current Lord Stepton," Mrs. Bennet chimed in. Everyone in the country knew about Lord Stepton, a gambler, spendthrift, and a pursuer of other men's wives. He had married the daughter of Lord Henley for the purpose of refreshing the Fitzwilliam coffers, and the union had turned out to be a disaster with their marital battles being fought in full view of the public.

Kitty related the couple's latest headline grabber. "Apparently, while guests at Marston Hall, Lady Eleanor went after His Lordship with a fireplace poker, and the earl ran and hid behind some drapes to get away from her."

"Ah, a Polonius assault," Lizzy said to everyone's amusement.

"I read about that chap as well," Mr. Bennet said. "Lord Stepton was with the Duke of Westminster when he led a raid using armored Rolls Royces against an enemy camp at Bir Hakkim in the Middle East where the crews of *HMS Moorina* and *HMS Tara* were being held. Grosvenor got the DSO for that exploit—not sure about Stepton—although I am sure he got something."

Knowing that Elizabeth was acquainted with the duke's first wife, Constance Cornwallis-West, from her time as a volunteer at the hospital in Le Touquet, Mr. Bennet looked to Lizzy to see if she had anything to add to his comment about the duchess as she was indebted to the great lady for an act of kindness. When Lizzy had become gravely ill with the flu in June of 1918, Her Grace had arranged for transportation to Boulogne for Elizabeth in her private car and had sent a maid with her for the journey to England and Hertfordshire. But Lizzy, who rarely commented on anything to do with the war, remained silent.

"Does anyone know if Mr. Darcy is with Mr. Bingley at Netherfield Park?" Jane asked, trying to lead the conversation away from the exploits of the married Bendor Grosvenor and Lord Stepton to the unattached Charles Bingley.

"I hope so," Kitty said, and started to giggle. "According to *The Tatler*, Mr. Darcy is a great, tall fellow, very handsome, and has dated all six of the English girls in the cast of *Floradora*."

"My goodness! All six!" Lizzy said, laughing. "He must be a most clever gentleman to juggle a half dozen women all at the same time."

"If that story is true, then Mr. Darcy is either a fool or very brave," Mr. Bennet said, winking at his favorite daughter.

"Mother, did Mrs. Long say if Mr. Bingley will be attending the dance?" Jane asked, continuing to press the issue of a single man in possession of a good fortune who might be in need of a dance partner. Jane had her answer when her mother broke into a big smile.

Chapter 3

After dinner, Jane and Lizzy paid a visit to Kitty's room where they found their younger sister pouring over the latest edition of *The Tatler*. After ten minutes of Jane beating around the bush, Lizzy finally asked the question her sister had been dying to ask. "Kitty, will you please tell us everything you know about Charles Bingley?"

Kitty hopped off her bed and pulled a box filled to the brim with old magazines from underneath the bed. On top of the pile were issues of *The Tatler* and *Inside London* that mentioned Mr. Bingley. Apparently, Kitty had already been hard at work mining the magazines for nuggets of information.

"You know that if Mary were still with us, she would chastise us for showing an interest in such tittle-tattle," Kitty said while thumbing through a magazine.

With Lydia married to an army veteran and settled near Newcastle and Mary having died nearly eighteen months earlier in the influenza pandemic, there were times when their younger sister appeared to be rudderless.

"But she is *not* with us," Lizzy quickly said, and realizing that her response sounded harsh, softened her tone and stated that although Mary was forever wagging her finger at her sisters for enjoying frivolous entertainments such as *The Tatler*, she always managed to stay in the room until every last detail had been revealed. "I really think it was her way of having her cake and eating it too."

"If only Mary had been here at Longbourn when you returned from France with the flu," Kitty said, looking at Lizzy, "she would have caught it just as everyone else in the family did, and when the next wave came, she would have had the same immunity as we did. It seems so unfair that because Mary went on holiday to Tunbridge Wells that she died."

"Kitty, life is full of what-ifs. What if Matthew Gardiner had stayed at Oxford for one more semester, he *would not* have been on the Somme on July 1, 1916 when they went over the top, and if Tim Smart had not had his appendix out that same summer, he *would* have been on the Somme. There are a thousand what-ifs, and since we cannot change the past, we must look to the future. My preference is to think that Mary is in heaven listening to this conversation and pretending to be outraged. So tell us, what do you know of Charles Bingley? Is he handsome? Is he really as wealthy as the Aga Khan? And most importantly, is he eligible?"

Upon learning the name of their near neighbor, Kitty had gone through back issues of *The Tatler* and *Inside London* and had discovered that there had been much speculation that Mr. Bingley would become engaged to Amanda Grenville, the heir to a department store fortune. Accompanying one article was a picture of Amanda, dressed in a full-length fur coat, waving goodbye to Lieutenant Charles Bingley as he boarded a ship bound for Belgium, and the young officer had responded by taking off his hat and waving it well above his head.

Jane practically grabbed the magazine out of Kitty's hand so that she might see what Mr. Bingley looked like, and what she saw pleased her. Lizzy, who was looking over her shoulder, nodded her head in agreement. The gentleman was handsome with a brilliant and inviting smile, and she guessed from the black and white photograph that he had blonde hair and blue eyes.

After retrieving her magazine, Kitty pointed out the most important facts regarding Mr. Bingley's relationship with Miss Grenville, specifically paragraph four, and Jane read it aloud: *Mr. Bingley lost a foot at Third Ypres, and although the couple took up where they left off upon Mr. Bingley's discharge from the service, it seems that Miss Grenville could not deal with the gentleman's infirmity as she dearly loves to dance.*

"There are always pictures of Miss Grenville in *Inside London* showing her dancing at the Ritz and the Savoy with a whole host of gentlemen," Kitty added.

"But how cruel of Miss Grenville to desert him because of a wound he sustained in the service of his country," Jane said, shocked that any one should treat a loved one in such a manner.

"Jane, I cannot tell you how many times I have witnessed such a scene while I was at St. Albans. And to be fair to these young girls and wives, they fell in love with one man, only to have a different person come home to them. We should not judge them too harshly."

"Perhaps I *am* being too harsh. But if Mr. Bingley is to attend the dance on Saturday here in Meryton that must mean he is still capable of dancing, so Miss Grenville's affections for the gentleman must have been very slight to have given up on him so easily."

Lizzy could have shared a hundred stories of love and loss that had come to her attention while volunteering as a VAD. There were women, like Miss Grenville, who could not bear less than a perfect mate and who turned on their heels and walked away from boyfriends and husbands without so much as a backwards glance. But there were also those who found their loved ones shorn of limbs or suffering from hideous injuries, but who refused to leave them, and because of their love, she had been a witness to miracles.

To Jane's disappointment, after Mr. Bingley's breakup with Miss Grenville, the only news Kitty had to share was that the gentleman had taken up the game of golf.

"Well, the good news is that he is ambulatory and likes to keep busy and stay fit," Lizzy said. Jane remained unimpressed. "It also means that if he had been seen around town escorting a beautiful lady, *Inside London* would have mentioned it," which cheered up her sister considerably.

"Although there isn't all that much about Mr. Bingley, there is item after item about his sister, Caroline." Kitty flipped through *Inside London* until she arrived at a page containing a picture of Miss Bingley on the arm of Freddie Jones, the son of the Sir Lloyd Jones, Baronet. "She was engaged to Mr.

Jones for about three months, but threw him over for a Swedish count. That's him right there. But apparently Count Frederickson's insistence that they live in Stockholm put an end to that engagement as well."

"She sounds rather flighty, doesn't she?" Jane asked Lizzy. "Two engagements since the end of the war."

"Well, when you are that rich and beautiful, I guess you can get away with being flighty," Lizzy answered while looking at a picture of a tall, thin, long-legged, long-lashed, exquisitely dressed lady of about twenty-two years.

"I think her circlet is made of diamonds," Jane said, squinting at the photo.

"Very likely. Just think how much money Bingley Iron Works must have made during the war." Lizzy failed to mention that these companies were known in the press as "merchants of death" and that many of them were being investigated for war profiteering, but she couldn't remember the Bingley firm as being one of those listed in the newspaper articles.

"This issue of *The Tatler* said that Bingley Iron Works underwrote all the expenses for an officer's club and dancehall in Knightsbridge during the war," Kitty said, holding up yet another issue in which

Caroline Bingley was prominently featured, "and Miss Bingley and Mrs. Hurst ran it for the Red Cross."

Jane looked out of the corner of her eye at Lizzy. She knew her opinion of high-society ladies who "did their bit" by dancing the night away with officers, but Lizzy always tempered her statement by commenting on ladies from the same tier of society who stood on freezing railway platforms handing out coffee and tea or holding a wounded soldier's hand.

"And now she is after this Mr. Darcy. I wonder what the gentleman thinks about being third in line?" Lizzy asked as she continued to study the picture of the stunning Caroline Bingley with her bobbed blonde hair, blue eyes, and long-fingered hands clutching a cigarette holder with a diamond band.

"I guess that all depends on whether or not Mr. Darcy is interested in Miss Bingley," Jane answered.

Chapter 4

"Lizzy, if you do not go to the dance, then I shall not go either," Jane said as she walked around their shared bedroom brushing her cropped blonde hair in preparation for bed. With Lydia now living in the North and Mary gone, the two oldest Bennet daughters could have had their own rooms, but they preferred to share a bedroom as they had always done. Since their childhood, sisterly discussions had been a part of their nightly routine, and with an eligible bachelor running loose in Meryton, there was much to discuss.

"But why must *I* go? You may go with Kitty or Diana Long. There is no need for me to attend."

"I don't understand why you won't go. You used to love to dance."

There was a time when Lizzy had liked nothing better than a dance, but at twenty-six, she found that she was often older than most of the males roaming the dance hall looking for partners. Naturally, the younger crowd would be drawn to the pretty Kitty and her friends, who were closer to them in age and who were willing to do some of the more risqué dances, such as the shimmy, that Elizabeth wouldn't be caught dead doing. There were other difficulties. Every time she went to a dance, she could not help but think of those who were no longer there to trip the light fantastic.

"I know that you complain about the lack of men of our age, but we now know that Mr. Bingley is in his late twenties and will be attending, and we also know that he has convinced his friend, Mr. Darcy, to go as well."

"And how do *we* know that?"

"I should be embarrassed to admit this, but I went for a walk this morning. My meanderings took me very near to Netherfield Park. When I saw Mrs. Smart in the yard hanging clothes on the line, naturally I struck up a conversation with her. She mentioned that Mr. Bingley's friend would be going to the dance."

"Did Mrs. Smart mention if Mr. Darcy had all of his appendages?"

"Lizzy!" Jane said aghast, especially since it was now known that Mr. Bingley had lost his foot at

Passchendaele.

"Sorry. Gallows humor."

Jane took her sister's hand in hers. "I know how deeply the war affected you, and you were so much braver than I was. I could never have done the things you did as a VAD to help those poor soldiers, but you really must try to look on the bright side of things. After all, it is the rest of your life."

"I do try, Jane. Honestly, I do. It is just that with John and Jeremy gone and Frank Hill in a wheelchair, it really is hard to enjoy a dance. They were my partners."

"But we must find new dance partners, such as Mr. Bingley and Mr. Darcy."

"But do we know if Mr. Darcy comes alone or in the company of six Floradora girls?"

"Lizzy, please," Jane pleaded.

"So you have set your cap for Mr. Bingley before you have even met him. Very well. I shall go to the dance because you have asked, and I shall have a good time because you have commanded it."

Jane nodded her head in agreement, and in doing so, revealed that she hadn't been listening to what Lizzy was saying. Rather, she was picturing herself dancing cheek to cheek with Charles Bingley.

* * *

It was just as Darcy had expected. The ratio of females to males was about five to one, and the claustrophobia that plagued him since his return from France hit him in the chest like a barreling wave. He didn't like crowds to begin with, but here, with all the ladies looking at him, he felt like a caged animal in a zoo. But eventually he must choose a partner. If he did not, in a neighborhood as small as Meryton, he would be roundly criticized, and his name would be mud by morning. He quickly scanned the faces of the ladies, and without robbing the cradle, he felt that Bingley was dancing with the only really pretty girl in the room. He decided to wait for the song to end, and then he would ask the lady to dance. But his plans were thwarted when Bingley immediately engaged her for a second dance, and so he stood apart, trying to look as if he was participating without actually dancing.

With the band now on break, Charles made his way over to his friend on the far side of the room. Unconsciously, Darcy had inched his way across the room until he was very near to the rear exit.

"Darcy, why are you not dancing? There are so many pretty girls here."

"Bingley, we agreed that you would not press the issue. Besides, you were dancing with the prettiest in the room," Darcy said. He was happy for his friend. Despite the prosthetic, he had acquitted himself quite well.

"Yes, Miss Jane Bennet is truly lovely, but her sister is very pretty as well."

Darcy looked around the room, but saw no one who bore any resemblance to Jane Bennet, and he abandoned the exercise when a gaggle of women thought he was staring at them.

"There is no one here to tempt me, Bingley. Please go and talk to Miss Bennet. Is that not the purpose of the exercise—to dance and to get to know your neighbors?"

"All right, Darcy, but look around. I am sure there is someone here for you. I am told that the next dance will be a foxtrot, and I know how much you enjoy that dance."

Darcy did look around and that is when he saw a dark-eyed beauty who had been standing behind him, but when he looked at her, she merely nodded her head and walked away.

Damn! Darcy thought. *She must have heard what I said. Now what? Should I ask her to dance or leave well enough alone? Well, I've been in worse jams than this.*

Lizzy watched as the gentleman made his way

towards her, and she correctly guessed that he was going to ask her to dance. *Great. My only dance tonight will be with someone who finds me unattractive and asks for a dance only at another's prodding.*

In Darcy's opinion, the lady was anything but unattractive. In fact, her beauty matched the most handsome women of his acquaintance. She had beautiful dark curly hair, and the curls framed a face with expressive dark eyes, an adorable mouth, and a dimple. After bowing, he introduced himself, and Lizzy extended her hand. "I am Elizabeth Bennet, the sister of your friend's dance partner, Jane Bennet."

Terrific. I have managed to insult a relation of the woman that Bingley can't seem to take his eyes off of. Good work, Darcy.

"Your sister is an excellent dancer, and in my friend, she has found a most agreeable partner."

"There is nothing that gives Jane greater pleasure than dancing. I can attest to the fact that before the war Jane received more dance requests than any other woman in our part of Hertfordshire. As we would say today, she 'cut a mean rug.'"

"And you? Before the war, did you cut a mean rug?"

"I had my share of dances, and there were few

complaints," Lizzy answered while appraising the Floradora man. She could easily understand why six actresses would fight for his attention. He was nearly six-feet tall, muscular build, thick dark hair, grey-green eyes, and a strong chin. All in all, he was a fine specimen of the male of the species. But there was something in the way he walked that made her think that he had suffered an injury, possibly to his back or hip, and there were definitely several small scars on his left cheek, possibly from diving into a hard surface. Because it had been part of her job for so long to evaluate a patient, she hardly realized that her staring at a man in such a way might be considered improper.

Well, she's certainly giving me the once over, Darcy thought as Lizzy continued to study him. *Maybe she's one of those liberated females who are always demanding the right to vote or equal rights in the workplace or some other such nonsense.*

Despite the inferior playing by the band, Darcy decided to give it a go and to ask the lady to dance. "Miss Elizabeth, after the band returns from break, would you like to dance? I understand that they are to play a fox trot."

Lizzy started to laugh, and then explained that the band only knew six songs, and three of them were fox trots. "When they return from their break, they shall begin again, but they are only boys just starting out and do the best they can." Remembering his comment to Mr. Bingley, she added, "Mr. Darcy, I suspect that you are merely being polite and really do not want to dance, and fortunately for you, I am not inclined to dance at the moment. So if you will excuse me."

As Darcy watched Elizabeth walk in the direction of the refreshment table, he wondered if he was more annoyed or embarrassed by her refusal. She had obviously overheard his statement to Charles about not wanting to dance and had taken it as a personal slight. But would it have killed her to have danced just the one dance with him? No, she could be as rude as he had been, and he made his way to the nearest exit.

* * *

As Lizzy watched Mr. Darcy leave, she unclenched her fists. *Why on earth did the man come to dance if he had no intention of dancing? Granted, the band was not the best, and an assembly hall from an earlier century suffered in comparison to the ritzy venues of London, but, honestly, when in Rome...*

Lizzy had little time to dwell on the missing Mr. Darcy because she was soon joined by Jane and Mr. Bingley, who graciously insisted that she call him by his first name.

"I thought I saw Darcy over here," Charles said, looking around the room for his friend.

"I believe he is out on the drive, possibly having a cigarette."

"Oh, Darcy doesn't smoke. He gave it up after he got out of... I mean, after the war, he stopped smoking. He is actually quite a crusader against the habit. Wouldn't leave me alone until I stopped. He particularly hates it when women smoke." Then not knowing if either Bennet sister smoked, he apologized.

"We do not smoke, Charles. I doubt that my father would approve," Lizzy said, answering for both. "But then we have never even tried. We are not so brave in the provinces."

"It really is a bad habit, but during the war, everyone smoked. I mean, it gave you something to do while you waited... because you were always waiting... for the next barrage or the next patrol or the big push. Something was always just down the road." Then Charles stopped talking. "Sorry about that. Rather depressing topic." He was rescued from further embarrassment by the band members returning from break.

"Elizabeth, may I have this dance?"

"I thank you, Charles, but I think your preference

is to dance with your first partner."

"Lizzy, stop that!" Jane said, her face aflame.

"Charles, my sister may pretend that she wants me to dance with you, but when we get home, she will cut into me for denying her a fox trot because there is no one in Hertfordshire who enjoys dancing more than Jane. Besides, you are one of the few couples who have actually managed to stay in time with the band, so get out there and dance."

The pair needed no additional encouragement, and they quickly returned to the dance floor. Lizzy soon found herself engaged for the next dance, an English tango, by the son of her father's law partner, a seventeen-year old boy, barely out of short pants. But what Todd lacked in skill, he made up for in enthusiasm, and Lizzy was flung about the dance floor with gusto.

When the dance was over, Todd offered to get her a cup of punch, an offer Lizzy eagerly accepted because she was completely out of breath. When he returned, she was treated to a steady stream of American slang as he was a great fan of detective stories shipped to him by a cousin from the States. As her partner "beat his gums," he complimented her on how "dolled up" she was, adding that she looked "spiffy."

"Thank you for the compliments. I took extra care with my hair tonight just in case I should meet a handsome gentleman, such as yourself," Lizzy said with a laugh.

"Says you," Todd answered. "I asked you to dance because I knew you wouldn't make fun of me if I couldn't do all the steps. You really are the bee's knees, Lizzy," and he pushed into her with his shoulder. "Did you get a load of that Silver Ghost out there in the car park? I wonder who has that much moola lying around to pay for that set of wheels?"

"The Rolls Royce belongs to Mr. Fitzwilliam Darcy, the grandson of the Earl of Stepton. It is my understanding that the family has so much money lying about the house that they stuff it into in vases and chests and hide it under chair cushions. When they go into town, they line their pockets with fistfuls of cash so that they might buy whatever takes their fancy." Then Lizzy started to laugh so that Todd would know that she was teasing him.

"Lizzy, you can't kid a kidder," and he let out a loud guffaw. "Unfortunately, I've got to get a move on it. I told my father I would have the car home by 11:00. I think he worries more about the Humber than he does about me."

"You know better than that, Todd," she said, scolding him, and then she asked him for a ride home.

But before leaving, she noticed that Mr. Darcy had reappeared and was looking at her with a smirk on his face, and she knew that he was laughing at her for refusing him, a handsome man, much nearer to her age, but agreeing to dance with a pimply-faced, lead-footed boy.

Chapter 5

Lizzy was already asleep when Jane came in, but that proved no deterrent to Jane's desire to talk about her evening with Charles Bingley. After pulling the chain on the bedside lamp, Jane moved the chair from the dressing table next to Lizzy's bed.

"Charles is everything a gentleman ought to be," Jane said, settling in nicely. "We fell into conversation so easily. It was as if we had known each other all of our lives."

Seeing the dreamy look in her sister's eyes, Lizzy realized that this might take awhile, and so she sat up, pulled her knees up to her chest, and tucked the blanket in around her in preparation for a full accounting of the night Charles Bingley and Jane Bennet first danced. Every detail of his attire, every *bon mot*, every kind gesture was shared. It was as if Lizzy had not been in attendance and had not seen how their eyes had locked in on each other from the moment Jane had come into the hall.

"Charles wants me to come to Netherfield for tea."

"My goodness, Jane! What an impression you have made. You will have him down on one knee in no time at all."

"Don't be silly. A man such as Charles, who can have any woman in British society, would not be interested in marrying Jane Bennet of Meryton. But I will confess that I do like him a great deal, so I shall take every opportunity to be with him. And of course, you will come with me to Netherfield so that I may do just that."

"Why would I go to Netherfield? Charles invited you, not me."

"You know that I cannot go alone."

"I know no such thing." When Jane pursed her lips, Lizzy did the same. "I cannot believe in this day and age that you would shock the neighbors if you went to Netherfield alone and in broad daylight, especially since every member of the Smart family, our friends and fellow church members, have been hired by Mr. Bingley for the duration. I am sure you will find a Smart in every room and one most definitely serving the tea. If you can manage to do anything improper with all those people milling about, I take my hat off to you and say go to it."

Jane and Lizzy had had numerous discussions about a modern woman's role in society with Jane always taking the side of the status quo, and she had backed up her belief that a woman's place was beside the hearth by remaining at home during the war, knitting balaclavas and rolling bandages. Even after the war had ended, other than the few hours she spent filing in her father's law office, she refused to take a job outside the home. In contrast to her conservative sister, Lizzy was full steam ahead—no holds barred. As far as she was concerned, other than serving in the military, women should run newspapers, attend university in co-educational classes, be surgeons and doctors, head corporations, play sports, and, most especially, have the right to vote.

"I beg of you, no discussion of women's right to vote. No songs of praise to the Pankhurst sisters. Not tonight," Jane pleaded. "Please."

Seeing her sister's distress, Lizzy pretended to lock her lips and to throw away the key.

"Did anything exciting happen after I left the dance? I mean, other than what you have already shared?"

"Well, I don't know if you would call it exciting, but Mr. Darcy danced with Sarah Dennison and

Diana Long. He seemed to enjoy himself, so I am surprised that he did not ask you to dance."

"He did ask. I refused him," Lizzy answered bluntly.

"Oh, Lizzy, please tell me that you are not serious. You said 'yes' to Todd Danbridge, but 'no' to Mr. Darcy?"

"Yes, I did, and I would do it again. Todd is an engaging partner."

"Who happens to be eighteen years old."

"I refused to dance with Mr. Darcy with good reason. He made it sound as if he was doing me a favor by asking me to dance," Lizzy responded with her jaw jutting out. "You should have seen the superior look on his face. He thought that he was above his company."

"I shall tell you that you have cut off your nose to spite your face," an exasperated Jane informed her stubborn-as-a-mule sister. "Mr. Darcy is an accomplished dancer, and when he danced the tango with Sarah, he whisked her about the room like a professional. Compare that to your experience with Todd. Unlike you, after Sarah had finished dancing with her partner, she had no holes in her hose."

Jane was correct. At every turn in Lizzy's tango with Todd, he had stepped on her feet.

"So what if it cost me a pair of hose? I had fun, and everyone has to start somewhere."

"It is now clear to me why you do not want to go to Netherfield Park. It is because you wish to avoid Mr. Darcy."

Lizzy slid under the covers. "We are both grownups. You can go to Netherfield without me, and I can survive being insulted by Mr. Darcy. Now, please shut the light. I need my beauty rest."

* * *

Although Lizzy and Jane had gone to bed upset with one another, it was impossible for the two sisters to stay that way. By the time Lizzy came down to breakfast, her resolve regarding her refusal to go to Netherfield was weakening. But when the phone rang, the matter was taken out of her hands.

The introduction of a telephone at Longbourn had been a fairly recent event, and because the novelty had yet to wear off, whenever the telephone rang, family members would gather around to find out who was calling. Thus, when Lizzy picked up the ear piece, everyone soon knew that someone from Netherfield Park was on the line.

"Good morning to you as well, Mrs. Paterson. Netherfield Park you say. Mr. Bingley for Jane! Well, let me see if I can find her." While Kitty giggled and

Mrs. Bennet beamed, Lizzy passed the telephone to her sister.

Jane had no sooner said goodbye than she was deluged with questions from her mother. With so few men of marriageable age in the neighborhood because of the toll exacted by the war, Mrs. Bennet was convinced that Lydia would be the only one of her girls to marry, but this sounded very hopeful and she must know everything.

"I have been invited to take tea at Netherfield Park on Monday at 3:00." After sharing her good news, she turned to Lizzy and granted her a reprieve. "Lizzy, you will not have to accompany me as two of Charles's sisters have come for a visit. When he arrived home last night from the dance, they were waiting for him, and they insisted that he invite me to tea."

"Excellent," Lizzy said, nodding her head in approval at Charles's quick work. "But I want you to know that I was going to agree to go with you to Netherfield. I was actually looking forward to it."

"Lizzy, it is a sin to tell a lie," Jane said, pretending to chastise her sister, but her frown was soon replaced by a smile, and Lizzy knew the reason why.

Chapter 6

"Lizzy, where have you been?" Mrs. Bennet asked her daughter before she was even through the door. Ignoring the raindrops clinging to her daughter's hat and coat, she continued to press. "When your father is away, we are quite stranded as you are the only one who knows how to drive the Renault."

"What do you mean, 'Where have I been?' I have been at the hospital working as I do every Monday from 8:00 until 5:00," she said, unbuttoning her coat revealing the uniform beneath.

"Do not take off your coat; Jane needs you. She has fallen down and has possibly broken her ankle."

"Where? How? I thought she was taking tea with Charles's sisters."

"I do not know all the particulars, only that she is injured and has asked that you go to Netherfield Park as soon as possible." Mrs. Bennet handed Lizzy a suitcase containing a change of clothes for Jane. "There is a frock in there for your sister that will do nicely for dinner."

"Has she been invited to stay for dinner?"

But her question went unanswered as her mother pointed her in the direction of the door with the instruction to "make haste, make haste."

"Before I go, may I please change my shoes?" Mrs. Bennet shook her head, denying her daughter's request. "But my shoes are dirty, and they have little pieces of gravel stuck in the soles."

"It is important that you go now as Jane called hours and hours ago. Besides, you can change into Jane's shoes as she will not be wearing them," her mother said, chuckling. "And once you have determined that her ankle is not broken, but merely sprained…"

"Mother, if there is any possibility that Jane has broken her ankle, then she will need to go to Watford where they have an X-ray machine."

"Nonsense. No one breaks an ankle falling off a step."

"Jane fell off a step? One step?"

"You must tell Jane that I insist that she stay overnight," her mother said, again ignoring Lizzy's question, "because she will not be able to put any weight on the foot, and it is best that she have her rest and to do so at Netherfield."

Finally, Lizzy understood. Since Jane could not walk on her own, it would be necessary for her to lean on Mr. Bingley, and in her mother's mind, leaning would lead to loving and a walk down the aisle in the village church.

* * *

Although a competent driver, Lizzy did not like driving in the rain, especially since the county roads had been sorely neglected during the war, and there were potholes everywhere. But because her father had gone to London for the day to meet with another solicitor regarding the probate of a will that was being contested by half the people mentioned in it, she had no choice.

By the time Lizzy started the Renault, the heavy rain that had started to fall during her ride home from the hospital had become a downpour. In order to avoid a huge puddle while turning into the south drive leading to Netherfield, she had turned the steering wheel too hard. As a result, the car had skidded, ending up in a swale and finally coming to rest at a precipitous angle. Because her dear Mama had pushed her out the door before she could collect her umbrella, she had to trek down the long drive with merely the hood of her coat for protection.

As Lizzy made her way to the house, she realized that it was not just the exterior of the house and the grounds that had been neglected by the Darlingtons, but the drive as well, and the ruts in the gravel had become twin rivers carrying all sorts of muck with a destination of the inside of Lizzy's shoes. When the door was answered by Tim Smart, he broke out laughing at the sight of a soaking wet Lizzy Bennet who looked more like a drowned cat than his childhood friend.

"Forgot your brolly and mac, did you?" he asked, handing her a dust cloth so that she might dry her hose.

"Stop laughing or I shall complain to the master and see that you are discharged immediately without a character," Lizzy said as she removed her sodden footwear.

"I swear it looks like you swam here," Tim said, thoroughly enjoying the sight before him.

"I did," Lizzy said, laughing. "I did the backstroke to keep the debris out of my mouth."

Any further merriment was prevented by the arrival in the foyer of Mr. Bingley's sisters, Caroline Bingley and Louisa Hurst. Both stared at Elizabeth as if she was not a drowned cat, but some repulsive creature that the cat had dragged in. After introductions were made, she was taken to her sister, who was sitting in the study with her leg propped up on an ottoman and cushioned by a pillow. If Lizzy resembled a cat or its prey, Jane looked like a mouse, all eyes and no voice, and one who wished she was anywhere but at Netherfield Park.

After Caroline and Louisa excused themselves so that they might make arrangements for the evening meal, Jane finally spoke. "Lizzy, I swear that if you tease me I shall burst into tears. I can't think of another time in my life when I have been more humiliated."

"Not even when you came running down the stairs in your slip just as a package was being delivered by Papa's handsome, young law clerk?"

"I was thirteen years old, and you don't forget anything, do you?" Jane grumbled.

Obviously, Jane did not find humor in this situation, and so Lizzy put on a serious face. "May I ask how this happened?" she said as she placed her hand on her sister's forehead.

Jane, who cried at the drop of a hat, described, through her sniffles, how she had gone around to the rear entrance of the manor house so that she might ask Mrs. Smart what she thought of Caroline Bingley and Louisa Hurst. But when she stepped up onto a platform that had once led to a now razed greenhouse, the rotted planks had given way. In trying to avoid a fall, she had twisted or broken her ankle.

After examining the foot, Lizzy rendered her diagnosis. It was her opinion that Jane had a badly sprained ankle as there was considerable swelling, and Lizzy could see her sister was in a fair amount of pain. It was Lizzy's experience that sprains were often much more painful than breaks. After propping up her foot with a second pillow, she rang for Tim and asked that he bring a cold compress. Once she was sure her sister was comfortable, she declared in a stentorian voice that the patient would live.

"But where is the master of the house?" Lizzy asked. "It would be such a shame if all of this suffering went unobserved."

"Very funny, Lizzy, but please note I am not laughing." But she then thanked her sister for coming so quickly, especially after having worked a full day at the hospital. "As for the whereabouts of Mr. Bingley, Charles and Mr. Darcy went to the chemist as there is not an aspirin in the house, and my foot is throbbing."

Lizzy took a bottle of aspirin out of her purse and shook its contents, and the rattling sound was music to Jane's ears.

"Well, I have instructions from Mama that you are to stay here tonight and not to come home until you are engaged," Lizzy said as she handed her sister a glass of water and the aspirin.

"I am *not* staying here. How would I get upstairs to the bedroom? Hop?" Jane shook her head at the absurdity of her predicament.

"Wasn't the point of your coming here to make an impression on the gentleman? Well, you have, and you have done it up royally. Besides, you won't have to hop. Charles will sweep you up in his arms and carry you to the nearest bed where he will linger as his eyes takes in the delights of your body. He might even climb into bed with you—just to provide some warmth, of course."

"Lizzy, such talk! I am shocked."

The sad thing was that Jane really was shocked, but after what Elizabeth had seen and the ministrations she had rendered during the war, there were few things that caused her to raise so much as an eyebrow. And what would her prudish sister think about some of the things Lizzy had seen while serving as a VAD in France, including walking past a brothel—a very busy brothel—with its emerging smiling faces every day on her way to the hospital at

Le Touquet?

While Lizzy was applying the compress to the swollen joint, there was a commotion in the foyer, signaling that the men had returned from their mission. Without premeditation, Lizzy's hand went to her hair in an attempt to tame any wayward tresses, and then she wondered why she had done that. She didn't need to impress anyone, most especially not Mr. Darcy. The two men entered the study with the Bingley sisters on their heels.

"Whose car is in the ditch?" Darcy asked.

"It is a swale not a ditch," Elizabeth answered. "I would not have driven a car into a ditch."

"Very well. Whose car is in the *swale*?"

When Lizzy explained how she had swerved to avoid the pothole, the gentleman looked more amused than sympathetic.

"I was just about to call the garage so that I might get my car out of the *swale*."

"No point," Darcy said. "The approach to the stone bridge between here and Meryton is flooded. We weren't able to go into the village to get the aspirin. It appears that no one is going anywhere tonight."

Chapter 7

Before dinner, Lizzy went to the powder room, and as soon as she looked in the mirror, she understood why Bingley's sisters had stood gawking at her as if she were an exotic, unshod specimen from the Amazon. Unlike most females between the ages of sixteen and thirty, Lizzy had opted not to bob her hair. If she had attempted the modern style, with her dense curls clustered about her chin, she would have resembled a circus clown. Instead, her long tresses, now free of all restraints, made her look very much like Medusa and equally as menacing. Because of the humidity, her hair was resisting every attempt to restrain it, and she finally pulled it back with a rubber band that she kept in her purse for just such an occasion.

There was also the matter of her uniform. Although she had removed the white apron, under it was a drab gray frock, making her look like a servant and completely out of place above stairs at

Netherfield Park. Her appearance in the dining room earned looks of disapproval from the Bingley sisters, but from Mr. Darcy, there was a quizzical expression that she was at a loss to interpret.

During dinner, Darcy could not shake the feeling that he had met Elizabeth Bennet before, and he was trying very hard to recall where, but without success. The irony was that after concerted efforts to suppress memories that had plagued him since the war, he was now trying to recall one. But he wondered if there was a memory to be resurrected or did Miss Bennet merely remind him of someone else? Considering that he had been in and out of hospitals for more than a year, it was probable that one of the dozens of nurses and aides he had encountered looked like Miss Bennet.

When the party adjourned to the drawing room, Lizzy was presented with additional evidence of just how far Netherfield Park had fallen. Because the Darlington children were so much older than the Bennet girls, Lizzy had entered the grandest house in the neighborhood on only a handful of occasions, but in her fertile imaginings, Netherfield Park had been a palace and she its princess. But no more. The once beautiful upholstery and carpeting were now threadbare, there was a slit in the leather ottoman that had been badly mended, the draperies were dingy and needed to be cleaned, if not discarded, and every room she walked through was in desperate need of paint. The house where her parents had danced and had fallen in love was looking very tired.

Noting Lizzy's expression, Charles acknowledged that there was a great deal to be done at Netherfield, but at the moment, he was working on repairing those things that had been deemed by a building inspector to be unsafe. "The platform out back, for example, must be removed," he said, and then he looked at Jane, the first person to suffer as a result of the lack of maintenance on the estate, but her smile reassured him. To Lizzy's amusement, nothing was said about her more recent accident on the badly rutted drive.

When Caroline heard that her brother intended to begin repairs on what she deemed to be "nothing more than a pile of bricks," she launched an assault of why every pound spent on the place would be a pound lost. "You would be better off razing the whole thing rather than trying to do repairs."

"Raze it! I would never do that. This is a wonderful example of mid-Georgian architecture, and one whose interiors were influenced by Robert Adam and the gardens by Humphry Repton."

"If there was ever an Adam influence, all evidence of his delicate taste has disappeared. Because of cigar smoke, his soft yellow is now an unpleasant mustard. There are water stains near the windows in the dining room, and those hideous drapes! I can't believe that they were ever in fashion. As for the gardens, you couldn't get through them with a machete." Caroline punctuated each charge against the Darlington estate with the dramatic use of her cigarette holder, its glowing tip adding periods to each sentence.

Her brother agreed there was much work to be done, but he insisted that even though Netherfield Park had seen better days, he liked the old brick house and added, "Besides, I like my neighbors." When he uttered that statement, he looked directly at Jane, and Lizzy had to stifle an "ah."

But Caroline had not yet tired of the subject and asked numerous questions about the former owners, intimating that they had tried to conceal the problems of the estate from its purchaser.

"Caroline, I knew exactly what I was getting when I bought Netherfield Park, and in a few cases, the Darlingtons brought areas in need of repair to my attention. If you had met them, you would have been impressed by both Sir John and Lady Darlington. They have seen more of the world than anyone I have ever met, and they are generous to a fault. Sir John was knighted because of his donations of some very fine artifacts from Bengal to the British Museum."

"Oh, my! Sir John was knighted!" Caroline said, laughing. "I doubt Fitzwilliam, who is the grandson of an earl, is impressed by Sir John being elevated to the knighthood. Are you impressed, Fitzwilliam?" she asked, forgetting that Darcy's own father had also been knighted.

What actually *did* make an impression on Darcy was the unkindness Caroline Bingley demonstrated by mocking people whom she had never met, especially since they had suffered the loss of both of their sons in Belgium, a tragic fact of which Caroline was aware, and there was no doubt in his mind as to the reason why she was directing her question to him. Now free of her Swedish count, she was once again on the hunt. But if she thought that he was going to be the next notch in her belt, she was sadly mistaken.

"Caroline, if you are asking what I think about titles in general, I would only say that you should think of some of the people who bear them, my cousin, Lord Stepton, for instance, and you will know my opinion on the matter."

Lizzy looked down at her lap. It seemed that she wasn't the only person whom Mr. Darcy didn't like.

"Miss Elizabeth, what is your opinion on titles?" Darcy asked.

"They are an ingrained part of our heritage,"

Lizzy said, shrugging her shoulders. It was a subject of little interest to her.

"That is a statement of fact. I asked your opinion." As she looked at his gray-green eyes, Lizzy felt as if he was trying to stare her down.

"I imagine that at some point they served a purpose—the Knights of the Round Table and all that."

"I sense that you disapprove of such things. Am I correct, Miss Elizabeth?"

Believing that he was deliberately goading her because he was annoyed at Caroline, Lizzy could feel her anger rising. "You are correct in sensing that I disapprove of something. But perhaps my disapproval is a result of impertinent questions asked by someone so new to my acquaintance." After returning his stare, she announced, "Anyone for bridge?"

Chapter 8

Despite her embarrassment, it was necessary for Jane to hop up the stairs to the guest bedroom, but her predicament provided some levity to a subdued evening. After Lizzy's comment to Mr. Darcy, the conversation had turned to non-controversial topics, such as the weather, opinions on the musical, *Irene*, then playing in the West End, and Mr. Hurst's contribution, a review of Edgar Rice Burroughs's novel, *Tarzan the Untamed*, with Lizzy suspecting that the rotund gentleman imagined himself as being cast in the leading role. Despite the inclusion of the subject of football, Mr. Darcy had nothing to add. Instead, he hung about the gramophone, changing the records as if it were his assigned station.

As soon as Lizzy and Jane were safely behind closed doors, Lizzy congratulated her sister on her conquest. "Jane, I honestly think Charles has fallen in love with you. Did you hear what he said to Caroline:

'I like my neighbors,' and then he looked right at you. My goodness! In short order, you will be consulting the calendar so that you might fix a date for your wedding."

"You are exaggerating Charles's interest in me," Jane said, standing on one foot and trying to maintain her balance while Lizzy helped her out of her frock. "Nevertheless, I am rather pleased with how the evening went—for me, at least. But that exchange between Mr. Darcy and you. My goodness, that was awkward."

"If Mr. Darcy thinks that by virtue of his position in society he has a right to know my thoughts on any given topic, he is much mistaken. I find the man to be rude and insufferable, and I have no idea what sin I committed to merit his enmity," she said as she pulled the bed covers back for her sister. "Didn't his mother or governess teach him that it is impolite to stare?"

"He was certainly staring at you."

"As if I were a specimen in the British Museum. Do you know how long he will remain at Netherfield?"

"All summer, I'm afraid. Because his mother and father are in France, he leased the house in town and stays with Charles when he is in London, and Mr. Darcy told me during dinner that although the Darcy

71

family owns a manor house in Derbyshire, it is undergoing extensive repairs. Because it is so close to the Peak District and the spa at Matlock, during the war, the Army used it as a retreat for officers who had served on the Western Front. He laughingly said that it must have been mandatory for all personnel to wear hob-nailed boots."

"Mr. Darcy laughed?" Lizzy asked incredulously. "I shall record it in my diary."

"Perhaps his being prevented from the use of his own home is the reason for his sour mood. In his unhappiness, he has given you the impression that he does not like you."

"Oh, I can assure you it is not merely an impression. But I don't care if he likes me or not. Although I find Mr. Darcy to be a puzzle, there is one thing that I can say with certainty. The gentleman from Derbyshire most definitely dislikes Caroline Bingley. In her case, the reasons are obvious: She is all fingernails and spittle, and although she thinks Mr. Darcy finds her comments to be amusing, it actually serves to further annoy him."

"I must agree with you there as I was witness to an unfortunate performance during tea. But I imagine Miss Bingley is used to having men fall over her, and she assumes Mr. Darcy will do the same. But in this, she is mistaken. As for his disliking you, I disagree.

All evening, he kept stealing furtive glances at you, and he had the most quizzical expression on his face. In fact, I got the impression that he was trying to figure out if he had met you before, and if so, when and where."

"Perhaps, it was at the Duke of Westminster's ball in Grosvenor Square last autumn. Don't you recall? Papa had to send to London for the diamonds."

"Lizzy, you are too funny," Jane said, laughing.

"Seriously, I have never laid eyes on the man, and I would remember if I had because, despite his unpleasant personality, he is very handsome. Actually, he is my ideal for a man: tall, dark, muscular, and according to you, a good dancer, so it is unfortunate that he is so unpleasant—not that he would be interested in me in any event."

"Again, I must disagree. I think Mr. Darcy *is* interested in you, and we may have an opportunity for more evidence of it. If this rain continues, we may have to stay here another night."

"Do not say that, Jane. I would rather swim Mill Stream than endure another evening of such company."

"But when you called Mother, she said that Papa had remained in London with our aunt and uncle because sections of the railway were under water.

Besides, you have endured worse things than a stay at Netherfield Park."

"Yes, but not since the armistice was signed," Lizzy said, sighing in resignation.

* * *

"Good grief, Darcy! I know you to be a fellow who speaks his mind, but your inquisition of Elizabeth resembled a frontal assault. No wonder she took umbrage at your question, and since when did you start caring about anyone's opinion about titles?"

"I don't give a damn about titles. My purpose in asking that question was to hear her voice. When she was conversing with Louisa about what shows are playing in the West End, I had a sense of *déjà vu*."

Charles started to laugh. "Darcy, you don't talk to *anyone* about the theater, not even your sister, so if you did have a conversation with anyone on that subject, you would most certainly remember it."

"No, you misunderstand me. It was not the subject that was of interest, but the lady. I am quite convinced that we have met before. I just can't think where."

"My guess is that she reminds you of one of your nurses or their aides. The memory was probably sparked when you saw Elizabeth in her uniform. But Elizabeth would not have nursed you because she was at St. Albans before joining the staff at the hospital in Watford, and you were in hospital in Derby and London."

"But it is more than just her voice," a frustrated Darcy said, and he stood up and started to pace. "It is her curly hair and dark eyes. In my mind, I see myself running my hand through her curls and looking into those black pools."

"Are you doing anything else with your hands?" Charles asked, laughing.

Darcy did not answer the question, preferring not to share with his friend that after he had retired on the night of the dance, he had taken Elizabeth into his bed, and the two had had a most pleasant time of it. But Charles and he were no longer adolescents at Cambridge, sharing their sexual, and unrealized, fantasies about women, and he would keep his dreams to himself.

"She is a damn attractive woman, and one of the few who is not a slave to fashion," Darcy continued. "The other night at the dance, she wore a dress with a braided belt, revealing a glorious waist, and one that showed a hint of a bust as well. Before the war, women showed their waists, and they used supports to accentuate their bosoms, on occasion, practically knocking a boy's eye out. I don't understand why these pin straight dresses are all the rage. They make women look like boys."

"I agree with you on that. I do like a woman to display her attributes, especially if she has long legs as Jane Bennet does. But to get back to Elizabeth, if you had met such a pretty lady before, surely you would remember her."

"One would think," Darcy said, biting his lower lip. "Well, I will not be satisfied until I recall who she reminds me of, and once I do, I shall seek the lady out and ask her to dinner."

Chapter 9

Lizzy looked out the window of Netherfield's drawing room, fully expecting to see an ark go by. Although the rain had stopped, the ground was saturated, creating an artificial lake on Netherfield's front lawn. There was one bright spot: Tim Smart had reported that the flooding near the stone bridge was the result of accumulated debris, and crews were working to clear it so that North and South Meryton might be reconnected. The workmen had told him that it should be finished by the following morning, but that meant another full day spent in the company of Mr. Darcy and Caroline Bingley.

Contrary to Lizzy's gloomy prediction, the afternoon proved to be more amusing than she could have hoped, with Caroline providing most of the entertainment. There was nothing that Mr. Darcy did that did not merit some comment from the lady. When he coughed, she asked if he was catching a cold, and when he sneezed, she quickly rummaged through her purse looking for a handkerchief before he could produce his own. And when he sat down at the desk to write a letter, she acted as if he was performing a task of great importance.

"Fitzwilliam, are you writing business letters? Such a dreadfully boring task."

"I am writing to my sister, Georgiana," Darcy said, talking over his shoulder and not bothering to turn around to answer her.

"How old fashioned you are. Most people would not trouble themselves but would pick up the telephone. But then you do have a beautiful hand," she said, practically purring.

"Georgiana and her husband have joined my parents in the South of France. They are leasing a country house where there is no telephone service other than one public telephone located in the village post office. If they did have one, I would most certainly ring them."

"Oh, please do send my best wishes to all of your family. I just adore them." The request produced a nod from Mr. Darcy, and he returned to his task. Silence reigned for all of a minute. "It has been too long since we were all together at Pemberley enjoying your excellent stables."

To make sure that Elizabeth knew that she had experienced something that Lizzy could only dream about, Caroline went on at length about rides around the lake or along woodland paths during Pemberley's glorious autumns.

"It will be a good while longer before anyone sees Pemberley again," Darcy interjected. "Because of the lack of materials and workmen, the repairs to the manor house are moving at a snail's pace. When you do visit, Caroline, you will be less than impressed with the stables as most of the horses were sold to the Army for the war effort, and they have not been replaced. Those remaining are there because they were rejected by the cavalry. I don't think there is a horse on the place that isn't at least ten years old."

Lizzy found much to parse in that communication. Obviously, Caroline had not been to Pemberley for at least two years or she would have known about the horses being sold, but then she would have been busy with her two fiancés and wouldn't have had the time. Secondly, Mr. Darcy was in no hurry to have Miss Bingley back to his country house or he would not have mentioned the inferiority of the present mounts stabled at his estate. For Caroline, her attempts to ensnare Mr. Darcy were not going well.

But there was only so much of Miss Bingley that Lizzy could take in one sitting, and after four rounds of gin rummy, the former VAD insisted that Jane needed to rest. Jane acquiesced, but she was not happy about it. Unlike her sister, she was enjoying her stay at Netherfield.

"Lizzy, why am I being punished because you are in ill humor? Charles and I were having a nice conversation when you interrupted us for the purpose of telling me, a grown woman, that I needed a nap."

"I didn't use the word 'nap,' I said 'rest,' and it is I who needed the rest. Doing so little is more exhausting than working in a hospital. I can't abide endless hours of nothing but talk, talk, and more talk with the prospect of even more talk this evening. If you weren't recovering from a sprained ankle, I would suggest a game of sardines, and I would drag Caroline into a dark closet and pinch her."

"Wouldn't you prefer to be in a dark closet pinching Mr. Darcy?"

Lizzy looked at her sister in alarm. It was almost as if she knew about the dream she had had last night in which she had crept into the gentleman's room and climbed into bed with him. After he had pulled her to him, they had kissed passionately, and then they had lain in each other's arms, protected from the world by the soft cover of darkness.

"I will admit that I wouldn't mind sharing a dark

closet with Mr. Darcy, but he must not utter a word because as soon as he did, something unpleasant would come out, and it would spoil the moment."

"I rather think he admires you. I do know that this afternoon when you were talking with Mrs. Hurst about *Irene,* he was listening to your conversation as if his life depended upon it."

"He did listen in on that conversation, didn't he? I wonder why, especially since he has previously indicated that he has little interest in musical theater. Perhaps, I shall tease him about it this evening."

* * *

That morning, when Lizzy had come down to breakfast wearing her uniform, the only frock she had with her, Louisa had offered Lizzy the use of her wardrobe, and since the offer was sincerely made, it was gladly accepted. At dinner, Lizzy's choice of a red dress was met with nods of approval from everyone, except Caroline. The younger Bingley sister was as class conscious as any daughter of a duke and did not approve of her brother's choice of friends and pretended to fool with her cigarette lighter when the comments about Lizzy's appearance were made.

In contrast to his younger sister's rude behavior, Charles was truly grateful for Louisa's gesture, especially in light of Caroline's inexplicable antipathy towards Elizabeth Bennet. Caroline's treatment of Jane had been less than warm, but it was nothing when compared to the cold shoulder she was giving Jane's sister. But he was the host, and such behavior would not go unpunished, and he bypassed Caroline, the superior musician, to ask Louisa to play something on the piano.

Her rendition of *Baby Won't You Please Come Home* and *Has Anyone Seen My Gal* had everyone tapping their feet, except Caroline, and singing the lyrics aloud, except Caroline, and applauding her efforts, except Caroline. Miss Bingley was clearly in ill humor, and when Charles requested *The Rose of No Man's Land*, Caroline had finally had enough.

"No one wants to listen to that maudlin ballad. I heard it often enough in the last year of the war at the officer's club. It had every officer practically crying in his beer. It is nothing more than sentimental tripe."

"Caroline, I made the request as homage to Elizabeth's service as a nurse during the war."

"Of that really isn't necessary," Lizzy said, immediately jumping in. "Besides, I wasn't a nurse, but a VAD." When Louisa looked confused, she explained that nurses were highly trained medical professionals who provided instruction and guidance for their army of volunteers, the Volunteer Aid

Detachments. "I do not wish to belabor the point, but it is important for people to understand that the two terms are not interchangeable. I could not have performed the duties of a nurse."

"As far as I am concerned, both nurses and VADs were angels of mercy," Charles said, "and I have been in enough hospitals to know what I am talking about."

"I agree with Charles that during the war nurses and VADs were angels," the formerly silent Mr. Darcy said. "In fact, I was visited by a real one." Now the gentleman had everyone's attention. "It was the middle of the night. I was suffering from the flu and was absolutely parched. I cried out for water, and this angel brought me a glass. I was so grateful that I took her hand, and she held it for the longest time. In gratitude, I placed my hand upon her cheek. She had been crying, and I wiped away her tears. Then something wonderful happened. I pulled her towards me and kissed her, and this beautiful creature kissed me back and allowed me to hold her in my arms."

Caroline started to laugh. "Fitzwilliam, I can assure you that you were either dreaming or were experiencing a case of wishful thinking."

"No, it happened," Darcy insisted. "And I think this angel of mercy saved my life. By this time in the war, I had despaired of it ever ending, and I didn't care if I lived or died. But when this angel came to me, I wanted to live because I wanted to find her."

"And did you?" a rapt Jane asked.

"No. When I awoke, she was gone, and when I asked the orderlies and VADs about this young woman with her dark luminous eyes, they told me that no one on the ward fit that description and that I had imagined it. But as I said, it *did* happen."

No one spoke until Lizzy said that she believed him, and all heads turned in her direction.

"I have heard such stories from other soldiers. In fact, there was a man on my ward who described in great detail the beautiful angel who visited him and who asked him to dance." When Lizzy heard Caroline's guffaw, she added, "They did the gallop right down the center of the ward." Everyone, except Caroline, laughed. "It is not an uncommon phenomenon," Lizzy continued, "especially for those who suffered with high fevers and others who were most in need of angels."

Darcy nodded his thanks for not ridiculing his recollection of an otherworldly visitor and then asked if she had been in France.

"Yes, but for such a short time. I was there only three months when I caught the first wave of flu in June 1918 and was sent home. When I recovered, I was assigned to the hospital in St. Albans. I never went back to France."

"In what hospital did you work?" Darcy asked, trying to maintain an evenness in his voice. Like his angel, Elizabeth had dark curly hair and dark eyes. Even in a darkened ward, the angel's eyes had shone like two circles cut out of the night sky, just like Elizabeth Bennet's. While waiting for her answer, he felt his mouth go dry as it had on the night his angel had visited him.

"Le Touquet."

Darcy felt his chest tighten. "In what ward?"

"I was in the casino on the second floor."

"Oh," and Darcy, who had fully expected her to say Ward 18, was overwhelmed by his disappointment, and he asked to be excused and immediately left the drawing room.

Chapter 10

After the evening at Netherfield, Darcy disappeared from Hertfordshire. The reason he gave Bingley for his hasty departure was that he needed to check on the repairs being made to Pemberley. What he did not share with his friend was that after believing for a mere moment that he had found his own particular angel in the person of Elizabeth Bennet, and upon learning that he had not, he had experienced a wave of melancholia that had sapped all of his energy, and he had fled Netherfield as if it were a house on fire.

After recovering from the flu in June 1918, he had returned to active duty, and in the closing days of the war, exploding shrapnel from a grenade had torn into his buttocks and hip. Most of the shards had been removed during the first two surgeries, but over the course of a year, pieces continued to work their way through his system, and in one case, had lodged in his lower back causing excruciating pain. Following the surgery, he had very nearly died of an infection. But during all the surgeries and hospital stays, he had held on to the belief that his angel was keeping watch over him. His remarks to that effect had led to a referral by his surgeon to the hospital psychiatrist who had tried to convince him that he had been in a state of delirium as a result of the fever associated with influenza. But then he would remember the taste of her lips, the curve of her breasts, and the feel of her body against his, and he knew that it was no fantasy. She was out there somewhere, and for a fleeting moment, he thought he had found her at Netherfield.

With Georgiana and his parents in France, Darcy roamed the halls of Pemberley and its gardens alone. But despite the comings and goings of the workmen and the accompanying noise, his own slice of Derbyshire, so near to the glories of the Peak District, had worked its restorative powers on him. After regaining his equilibrium, he had returned to Netherfield Park to visit with Charles prior to his returning to Cambridge to take up his study of the law. He was relieved to learn that Caroline had left soon after his departure and had pressured her sister and her husband into coming with her.

During the weeks of his absence, Charles had been busy on two fronts: repairing the rear and front entrances to the manor house and romancing Jane

Bennet. When Bingley met him in the drive, he was informed that he would soon be asking the lady to become his wife, and the joy on his friend's face was contagious. Darcy felt the return of a lightness of heart that he always associated with being in Bingley's company. Even under the worst of circumstances, as when he was being fitted and refitted for yet another artificial foot, it was Bingley who had held steady, reassuring his friend that the pain was manageable, and the man's stiff-upper-lip attitude had proved to be an inspiration during some of Darcy's darkest hours.

"You couldn't have come at a better time," Charles said. "On Friday, there is a dance at the hotel in St. Albans, and Jane, Elizabeth, and I shall be going. If you come along, we can go on a 'double date' as the Americans call it."

"Well, I would like to go, but let us not call it a date. Elizabeth Bennet is not overly fond of me."

"Oh, but you are wrong. She asks after you all the time. When you left Netherfield so suddenly, she thought that you might be ill and was very concerned. I told her the real reason for your departure—you seeing to the repairs at Pemberley—and she was happy to hear it."

"In that case, I agree."

* * *

Lizzy was a reluctant double dater. She hardly knew Mr. Darcy. In fact, they were still using the formal terms of address of Mr. Darcy and Miss Elizabeth. Yet, here she was sitting next to the gentleman in the front seat of his Rolls Royce on her way to a dance at St. Albans. She had only agreed to go because she desperately wanted to dance with a man who knew the steps to all the latest dances. As much as she loved Todd Danbridge and all the other local boys, they were lead foots when compared to Charles Bingley and, according to all reports, Mr. Darcy as well.

The ride to the hotel had been pleasant enough. When Charles was not talking, Mr. Darcy had made an attempt to engage Lizzy in conversation. By the time they had pulled up to the hotel entrance, he was addressing her as Elizabeth and had asked that she call him William.

Because the St. Albans Hotel was known to have excellent bands, there was a crush of people waiting at the door to pay the admittance fee. As a result, a warm night was made all the warmer by the heat of too many bodies in too small a space, and Lizzy detected an uneasiness in William's demeanor. As soon as they went into the ballroom, William went to the bar and returned with a white wine for his date and two fingers of whisky for himself. After quickly polishing off the whisky, he headed back to the bar for another. If this continued, Lizzy knew that either Charles or she would be driving the Silver Ghost home, and her heart sank at the thought of dancing with an inebriated man. But her worries were soon put to rest. William put his second drink down and extended his hand so that he might escort Lizzy to the dance floor where the master of Pemberley executed a perfect tango, and she thought that she had died and gone to dance heaven.

After dancing a fox trot and waltz, Lizzy said that all the exertion had left her in need of a glass of water, and William stopped and stared at her. "What did you say?"

"I said that I needed a glass of water," and Lizzy watched as the color drained out of his face. "William, you are unwell," she said, gently placing her hand on his arm. "Please go outside onto the terrace immediately, and I shall bring you a glass of water." She pointed him in the direction of the exit.

When Lizzy joined him on the terrace, Darcy was wiping his face with a handkerchief and looking vulnerable and unsteady. She understood what had happened as she had been a witness to such scenes at the hospital on numerous occasions. Some sight, smell, or sound would trigger a memory, causing a sense of disorientation. She had learned that the best response was for her to establish a physical presence by touching the patient with her hand and just listening.

"Sorry about that. Ever since I was wounded, these 'episodes' as my doctor calls them occur every now and then. It usually happens when I am around a lot of people who are unknown to me. I feel as if the room is closing in, and I… I panic."

"It is actually quite common amongst soldiers who have been in the trenches to have these attacks. I attended a symposium at the hospital in St. Albans hosted by a disciple of Dr. Rivers from Craiglockhart in Scotland. Dr. Ambrose said that in unfamiliar situations the brain senses a threat, such as one would experience during wartime. But since there really is no danger, the brain becomes confused, and in its confusion, a sense of panic ensues."

"That sounds logical. And I am familiar with the work of Dr. Rivers. My brother-in-law was at Craiglockhart for six months, and he found Dr. Rivers' regimen beneficial. Even so, he can't abide the noises of modern society, and he and my sister are living in a villa in the country near Aix in Provence. My parents are visiting them, and during the Christmas break, I shall join them."

"I understand Provence is famous for its cuisine

and scenery. It seems that it would be the perfect place to recover."

"It is beautiful in an austere way."

"You mentioned a Christmas break. What did you mean?"

"Before the war, I had been studying the law at Cambridge. I wanted to be a barrister, but the war scuttled all my plans. I was hiking in the back country of Australia when news reached me that war had been declared. Because of U-boat activity, it took me nearly four months, traveling by a most circuitous route, to get back to England. By the time I arrived, Bingley had already enlisted and that is why he ended up in Belgium while my regiment was sent to France." After realizing that he had brought the conversation back to the war, he stopped talking. Placing his hands on her arms, he turned Lizzy so that she was facing him and asked, "Elizabeth, have we ever met before?"

"No. I am sure that I would remember if we had."

"But you were at Le Touquet," he said, his eyes boring into her.

"From the first day of my arrival to the last, I was in the casino, but you were not."

"No. I was in one of the temporary wards. It is just that you seem so familiar to me, especially your voice. Every time you speak, I find myself reaching out, trying to grab hold of a… mirage."

"William, you have been in and out of hospitals for two years, and in that time, you have met many VADs and nurses, and we all speak in our best hospital voice: soft and soothing. Honestly, we really all do sound alike."

"Well, if you had been an aide working on my ward, I most certainly would have found your voice to be comforting. I am sure you were an excellent VAD."

"Not really. Every day was a struggle. A good VAD and, more importantly, a good nurse acts on her instincts. She knows what to do in any given situation. That was not the case with me. I needed so much direction, and when there was a push and the casualties were high, I always felt as if I was running hither and yon to no purpose."

"To no purpose? I doubt that very much. I know those sisters, and if you did not do your job properly, they would have sent you packing without giving it a second thought."

"Yes, that is true. They cared only about the patients, and they let you know that at every opportunity."

"You said that nursing was difficult for you, and

yet you continue to nurse."

"Reluctantly. Immediately after the war, there was such a need that I stayed on at the hospital in St. Albans, working three days a week, and two in my father's law office. After things settled down a bit, I cut back my hours to two days and then to just the one day and took a position at the hospital in Watford to be nearer to Longbourn. I intend to resign in the new year. By that time, they will have ample staff to handle the case load. But no more talk of war or nursing. If you do not wish to go into the ballroom, we can stay out here."

"I would like that."

"But I would like to say just one more thing," Lizzy said, as she took the handkerchief out of William's hand and wiped his brow. "Your angel of mercy may not be a person at all, but a symbol of a secure place, a sanctuary, where you are safe from harm."

"You're probably right, and if she really did exist, what are the chances that I would ever find her again?"

Chapter 11

After returning to Longbourn, Jane was too excited to sleep, and as they had done when they were in their teens, they stayed up late talking about the handsome men who would come into their lives and sweep them off their feet as Charles Bingley had done. According to Jane, Charles Bingley was practically perfect in every way: kind and considerate, a fine dancer with a lovely voice, as well as having an exuberant spirit and a contagious laugh, and everyone knew that there was no one who could tell a joke quite like Charles, which Lizzy had to admit was true. With Charles's start and stop delivery, it was always a relief when the punch line was finally delivered.

But what endeared Charles to all of the Bennets was how over the moon he was about Jane and how he wanted everyone to know it. When Lizzy saw the two together, it gave her such joy to know that at least one of her sisters would find happiness in marriage as it most certainly wasn't Lydia whose hastily-arranged marriage to an Army corporal was failing. She preferred to think about William Darcy.

After William's panic attack in the ballroom, understandably his preference was to remain on the terrace away from the crowds, but that didn't mean that they couldn't dance. And dance they did, weaving their way around tables, chairs, potted plants, and other obstacles, until a crowd had gathered. After acknowledging a round of applause for their exhibition, the couple had walked into the conservatory to continue their conversation, and the first thing out of William's mouth was an invitation for Lizzy to come to Pemberley when the repairs to the manor house were finished.

"Progress *is* being made, but it is the slow-but-steady kind that can be quite maddening. As you can imagine with all the shortages of material because of the war, it is difficult to get wood and copper wiring and bathtubs..."

"Bathtubs?"

"Believe it or not, at Pemberley, this great country manor house, there were only two bathrooms above stairs, which was a problem because my sister would take hour-long baths, and my mother was also inclined to spend a good portion of the morning soaking in her tub. The house is more than 200-years old, so it is quite a challenge to modernize such an old house. For example, although the public rooms on the ground floor were electrified, no modern heating system was installed. The only heat comes from soot-clogged fireplaces. On the other hand, the private rooms on the first floor have radiators, but they aren't up to the task of heating such large spaces. So in the winter, we huddle together in an upstairs sitting room, reading by candlelight. It makes for a… Why are you laughing at me?"

"I had no idea that being rich was so awful." William gave her such a look, but it did not stop her from laughing at his expense. "Besides, there are advantages to living as our grandparents did without all of these modern conveniences. Huddling can be a good thing," Lizzy said, and she was rewarded with a half smile, one of William's most endearing traits.

"Did you say cuddling?"

"No. I said huddling—as Rugby players do—or as Darcys do on a cold winter's day."

"Oh, that's too bad. I'll take cuddling over huddling any day. But I was speaking of my difficult life at Pemberley. Before my father left for France, he handed over the management of the estate to me. Because he had relied on rents for the bulk of the family income, ends were not meeting. As I'm sure you are aware, while income and property taxes have risen, agricultural prices have been in decline for decades. Fortunately, Bingley had convinced me years ago to buy shares in his company, and profits from that investment has been paying the bills at Pemberley, that and selling off eight parcels of 250 acres." When Lizzy looked surprised to hear of the sale of any part of the Darcy legacy, he elaborated. "It is no longer possible to maintain these vast estates, and, frankly, I don't want to."

"I read in the newspaper that the Duke of Devonshire has sold Devonshire House in London to a developer," Lizzy said, "and that they are going to demolish it."

"No loss there. The exterior is hideous, and the interior is so garish that it's the equivalent of a second-rate hotel in Brighton. His Grace told me that the contents of Devonshire House will be moved to Chatsworth and to the Cavendish townhouse at Carlton Gardens. Even for the Cavendish families, economies must be made as there are tax bills to be paid. They have already parted with Shakespeare's folios and other priceless books from their library. My point is that the style of living of my grandparents' generation is no longer supportable, and so I am taking steps now so that I will never find myself in a position where I am forced to sell the Shakespeare quartos in my family's library to pay Inland Revenue.

"But I don't want to give you the impression that the Darcys are living hand to mouth. In addition to

Pemberley and a house in town, we do have a lovely villa near Eastbourne, and there is a funny story that goes along with it. You may have heard that during the war Lord Kitchener established a hospital for the Indian soldiers at Brighton Pavilion. My family was asked if our villa could be made available to the Indian doctors for their use as a retreat. These particular doctors were of the Hindu faith and could not eat meat or anything that had come in contact with meat, and so it became necessary for the army to provide them with their own housekeeper and cook. And that is a long way 'round to ask you if you would like to come with me to Eastbourne—Jane and Charles, as well. Of course, we shall be properly chaperoned as our former cook and butler reside there."

"Are you implying that I will need someone to protect me from your advances, William?" Lizzy asked, laughing.

"You might," and he placed his hand on hers.

* * *

Lizzy listened to the sound of Jane's breathing and wondered what Charles would think when he discovered on his wedding night that his wife was a heavy breather who was given, on occasion, to bouts of snoring. After finally saying all that there was to say about Charles Bingley, Jane had turned over on her side and had fallen asleep, leaving Lizzy to her thoughts, and her thoughts were of William.

As she pondered all that he had shared, his claustrophobia, the finances of Pemberley, his seaside villa in Eastbourne, she wondered why he had done it. Could it be that their relationship had changed course when he had confessed at Netherfield that he had been visited by an angel and that she had believed him? But there was a reason she did not doubt him: She, too, had been visited by angels. The first had appeared shortly after Jeremy had died. After leaving her friend's side, an angel had called out to her and had insisted that she rest in one of the hospital beds, and she had lain beside him and had fallen into a deep sleep with his arms encircling her.

After leaving Ward 18, she had returned to the casino and reported to Sister McCrory. As soon as Sister saw her, she knew that she had come down with the flu and ordered that she be put into isolation where her condition rapidly deteriorated. The Duchess of Westminster, believing that Elizabeth was so gravely ill that she might not live, had arranged transportation for the young VAD to return to England. The days that followed were mere blurs, but Lizzy remembered a different angel had come to visit her while she was in a hospital near her home. But she was not frightened because she had seen how content Jeremy was to leave the ugliness of this world behind. She only grieved for her family. But then the angel turned away, and she knew that she would live.

Mentally and physically exhausted from war and illness, Lizzy's recovery had taken months. When she was well enough to return to duty, she was assigned to the hospital in St. Albans. Within the month, a plague descended on the land in the form of another, more virulent influenza. Because she had some immunity, her services were much in demand, and when her mother had written to her, pleading with her to return home to care for Mary, she said that she could not leave her patients. She did the best she could for those in her care, but mostly she eased their final moments. Nothing she did—nothing anyone did—seemed to change the outcome. It wasn't until the fury had passed on its own terms that the crisis had ended, and by then, more than 20 million people worldwide were dead, including Mary Bennet.

But William and she had not been amongst the numbers of those lost in the war or in the pandemic. And maybe that was the bond between them. Both had survived the Apocalypse.

Chapter 12

From the time William had taken her into his arms at the dance at the St. Albans Hotel, Lizzy realized that she was in danger of falling in love with Fitzwilliam Darcy, and she knew that she was heading into troubled waters. She was less concerned with the differences in class and life experiences than with the idea of loving a man who was in love with another woman, a woman who happened to be an angel. She would be playing second fiddle to a phantasm.

While Lizzy proceeded with caution, Darcy was full steam ahead, and in the waning weeks of summer, he had done everything he could to reassure her that he was in love with the very real Elizabeth Bennet. He understood that the best way to put her mind at ease was not to talk about his angel. Although he remained silent about the night in the French hospital, he found that he was able to share much of that part of his life that he had kept secret: the horrible things he had experienced during the war.

"Before going to France, I actually placed a great deal of emphasis on my position in society, and a lot of other rubbish as well. But the best man I ever knew was my master sergeant who grew up in the slums of Liverpool and had used the army as a way to leave the gutter behind him. Sergeant Sullivan had the most appalling Scouser accent, and when he gave his report, my condescension for his lower-class origins was obvious. But he had so much to teach me, and as the months went by, my respect for him grew to the point where I considered him to be as noble as any of Arthur's knights, that is, if Knights of the Round Table swore like a public house brawler. I mentioned him so often in dispatches that it provoked comment at headquarters, but I didn't care. I knew the man was a hero, and his deeds would be acknowledged if I had anything to do with it.

"It is because of Sergeant Sullivan's bravery that I am here today. It was he who absorbed most of a grenade blast that would have killed me if he had not jumped in front of it. Fate has taken the better man." William started to cry, and Elizabeth's quiet acceptance and understanding of the burden he carried proved to be cathartic. Without fear of being judged or reproached, the story of Sergeant Sullivan's death had opened a flood gate for other tales of bloody battles, men lost, victories won, and how the war had changed him irrevocably.

But even before he had bared his soul to her, Darcy knew that he was falling in love with Elizabeth. He could almost trace the first tug at his heart to watching her tend to her sister at Netherfield in her stocking feet. Despite eruptions of steam from the radiators, like everything else at Netherfield Park, they performed inadequately, and the room was chilly. But the former VAD had a patient to care for and had set aside her own comforts to see to her sister. He felt the second tug when she had stood up to him regarding the matter of titles. She would defer to no one, and he liked her pluck. But it was at the dance at St. Albans, when he had taken her in his arms, that he knew he was in love because there was a familiarity there that was comforting, and so their courtship had begun with that first dance.

After picnics on Longbourn's lawn, evenings spent together at Netherfield, dining with the Bennets, or riding bicycles into Meryton, their feelings would not be denied, and they would seek each other out at every opportunity. In return for Darcy indulging her love of croquet and tennis, Lizzy agreed to take up the game of golf and had learned the language of the course, especially the term "bogie." But because she worked in her father's law office on Tuesday through

Friday and at the hospital on Monday, William must wait for her, and he could be found sitting in his Silver Ghost out front of the hospital or idling at the curb near Bennet & Danbridge, Attorneys-at-Law, four days a week.

In those weeks, Lizzy discovered that the master of Pemberley had a sense of humor. She had teased him about courting all six Floradora girls and pretended not to believe his explanation.

"John Moncrief invited me to join him for dinner at the St. Regis. When I arrived, he was entertaining five of the six Floradora girls. It was obvious that I had been invited for the purpose of footing the bill. Rather than embarrass him, I picked up the tab, and for my generosity, I was repaid with a mention in that rag, *Inside London*."

"Hmmm" was her only response.

But then it was her turn to be teased, and Darcy told her that it was not true that the Darcys stuffed cash under their chair cushions. "We neatly stack our money and place it in the safe next to the diamonds and rubies," he explained. Lizzy turned beet red when she realized that he had overheard her conversation with Todd Danbridge, but then she burst out laughing.

Darcy kept his promise and whisked Lizzy away to Eastbourne for a long weekend with Jane and

Bingley in tow. In a scene demonstrating the mingling of cultures during the war, as soon as they entered the Darcy villa, they could smell remnants of the exotic scents of its former Indian inhabitants. But they were also greeted by Mr. and Mrs. Jackson, the quintessential British couple, both wearing cardigans and sturdy shoes, who had retired to Eastbourne after a lifetime of service to the Darcy family as their butler and cook.

After walking into a bracing wind and fighting the midsummer crowd for a space on the beach wide enough to spread a blanket, Darcy suggested that they go on a picnic farther inland. To Lizzy's surprise, Jane and Charles declined, and Lizzy wore a puzzled expression until Darcy whispered that the couple wished to be alone. After returning to the villa where Mrs. Jackson whipped up a picnic lunch, they were off kicking up dust on country roads while looking for a good location for a picnic for two. They finally stopped and asked a farmer's wife if they could have a picnic in her meadow. After Darcy had offered her a gratuity, she agreed. They soon found the perfect spot, and immediately abandoned it for a walk down a country lane with Lizzy's hand firmly in William's grasp.

"I am really surprised about Jane staying behind," Lizzy said. "She is so conservative. When Charles invited her to tea at Netherfield, she told me that she would not go if I did not."

"So I am in Jane's debt as it is she who has enabled us to finally be alone. As fond as I am of Charles, he does talk an awful lot," William said, while swinging Lizzy's arm in a wide arc. "And because he is my dear friend, I am happy that he has found your sister. I was worried that he would end up with some gold digger. His problem is that he's too nice, and people take advantage of him. When we were at Cambridge, it was a real problem. Someone always had their hand out, and he rarely said 'no.' But Caroline is the worst. Knowing of her habits and being the executor of his father's estate, Charles saw the necessity of putting his sister on an allowance. But she's always on the telephone ringing him up looking for more money."

"You don't like her at all, do you?"

"No, I don't. You would think that with all her brother has experienced that she would be a little more considerate, and it's not just Charles. At the start of the war, while I was still on my way home from Australia, their brother, Dennis, died on the retreat from Mons, and their sister, Esther, died in the epidemic."

"I don't care for Caroline either," Lizzy answered, "but I think you are being a little hard on her. Her excessive spending may be a way of covering up the hurt she feels as a result of her losses. I am sure she lost many friends. It may help her to forget."

"Forget? It's a fool's errand," Darcy said, shaking his head. "Those things are burned into your brain. The most you can hope for is that over time the vivid images will blur and not rise up like some colored version of a phantasmagoria."

"I am going to disagree with you," Lizzy said, gently placing her hand on William's arm. "I have known men who have managed to forget the most horrific scenes. I believe that there are some things that are so jarring, so outside one's experience, that a person is quite capable of pushing unwanted images or events into the farthest reaches of one's mind where they remain locked away until disturbed."

But Lizzy's explanation did not satisfy Darcy, and as they made their way back to the blanket, he continued to grumble. "I didn't like her before the war either—Caroline, I mean."

"I am not surprised, and I believe it was your dislike of that lady that caused you to be so rude to me at the dance and later at Netherfield?"

"I? Rude to you? I beg to differ. I asked you to dance, and you showed me your back."

"And your response was to walk out the door in a

huff. There were other ladies at the dance who were in need of a partner."

"Other than Jane, who was dancing with Charles, there was no one there for me."

"Nonsense! My sister, Kitty, was there with her friends.

Darcy shook his head. "I couldn't ask her. What is your sister? Nineteen? Twenty?"

"She is twenty-one."

"Well, she looks younger. Elizabeth, you must understand that for me there is a demarcation line separating those who experienced the war and those who did not. If you didn't undergo some hardship, how can I talk to you? And so I avoid social situations with people who escaped the madness because how would they ever be able to understand me." No more was said on the subject, but Darcy took her hand and brought it to his lips and kissed it. And Lizzy wished that he would do more.

* * *

Looking all about her, with cows lowing and dragonflies buzzing a nearby pond, Lizzy told William that she felt as if she had stepped into a Constable landscape. "I fully expect a maid carrying a yoke of milk to come walking down the lane."

"Do we not deserve such a serene landscape?" Darcy asked, tossing her an apple from the picnic basket.

Lizzy agreed that they did, and she came and sat next to him on the blanket. After taking the fruit from her hands, he lay down and pulled her with him. He placed his arm around her waist and brought her to him so that there was no space between them, and their lips met. He felt the heat caused by her kisses coursing through his body, and he gently moved against her savoring her responses to his touches.

At first, Darcy thought that he had never experienced anything so wonderful, but then he moved away from her. The truth was that he had experienced something equally wonderful, and he was overwhelmed with the memory of his angel lying beside him in his hospital bed at Le Touquet, and he sat up. Lizzy saw the change, the look of confusion, and understood the reason.

She encouraged him to place his head on her lap, and after turning in to her, he wrapped his arms about her hips. While running her fingers through his hair so that she might purge all unwanted thoughts, she whispered, "If you do not quit on me, I shall not quit on you. I promise you that," and she kissed his head. He nodded, but continued to cling to her in silence.

The words Lizzy had whispered were not merely

meant to comfort. She was now so in love with Fitzwilliam Darcy that she was willing to do anything, including sharing her love for him with a ghost.

Chapter 13

Few families in Meryton had done more for the war effort than the Lucas family. While John and Jeremy had marched off to war, James and Jacob had gone to work in a munitions factory and their sisters in hospitals. Only the Darlington and Lucas families had received two telegraphs from the War Department, explaining that their sons had made the ultimate sacrifice on behalf of their country. The only difference was that the Darlington boys had died early in the war, and Lord Kitchener "had sent his sympathy." But with Kitchener at the bottom of the North Sea, the telegrams to Mr. and Mrs. Lucas had been signed by David Lloyd George.

As was the custom of the British army, the Lucas sons were buried where they fell, and so John lay in Monte Piana in Italy and Jeremy rested at the Communal Cemetery at Le Touquet in France. But their service would be acknowledged, and Mr. and Mrs. Lucas had led a fund-raising campaign to erect a monument in memory of all those from Meryton who had given their lives in The Great War. On this beautifully sunny August day, the sixth anniversary of the beginning of the conflagration, friends and family had gathered for its unveiling with the official dedication to take place on Armistice Day, November 11, 1920.

The crowd was so large that the constabulary had to redirect traffic away from the center of town, and many of the motorists, realizing what was taking place, had parked their cars and had joined the commemoration. Among the throng were Charles Bingley and Fitzwilliam Darcy, who stood to the rear of the crowd so that those who had suffered the loss of their friends and neighbors might be closer to the memorial.

The brilliant sunlight contrasted with the purpose of the day, but with eighteen months now gone since the cessation of hostilities, wounds had begun to heal. After all the speeches were made and the names read, stories about the shenanigans of the Lucas boys, Adam Hill, Patrick King, Stephen and Edward Darlington, and Bobby Long were shared. Lizzy had begun the reminiscences by declaring that if Jeremy Lucas had pulled her braid one more time that she would have cut it off, and a teary-eyed Jane spoke fondly of her first kiss—on the cheek, of course—from Patrick King. Jimmy Long laughed at Jane naming her first suitor, stating that his brother Bobby had claimed that he was the first boy to kiss the beautiful Jane Bennet, which caused a gentle laughter to roll through the crowd.

At the conclusion of the ceremony, all were invited back to Lucas Lodge for cake and punch, and it was there that Lizzy was reunited with her dearest friend, Charlotte Lucas. Unlike Lizzy, who found every facet of nursing to be difficult, Charlotte was a natural, and during the second year of the war, she had been encouraged to undertake the arduous training of a nurse. Even when the guns went silent, her services were needed as she was also an excellent teacher, and the hospital had asked her to stay on and train others who would care for the multitudes of wounded in their care.

Charlotte had brought with her from London several of her nurses-in-training, and Lizzy was introduced to Mary Paget, who was the outstanding graduate of her class of nurses.

"So tell me, Mary, is Charlotte a tough taskmaster?" Lizzy asked.

"She is indeed, but she is also the best person to train under in the whole of London. I never thought that I would become a nurse, and there were many times when I despaired of completing such a rigorous course, but Sister Lucas got me through it."

"And Sister Lucas must excuse herself as I have guests to thank for coming today," Charlotte said, nodding her head in the direction of Mr. Bingley and Mr. Darcy. Her purpose was to introduce herself to the gentlemen and to thank them for attending the ceremony.

"It was a privilege to have attended the ceremony," Charles said to Charlotte on behalf of both gentlemen.

"May we offer our condolences for the loss of your brothers," Darcy added.

"I can hardly believe it is three years since my eldest brother John was killed in Italy, and we are now gone past the second anniversary of Jeremy's death on the Marne. Actually, he was not killed on the Marne; he died in hospital in Le Touquet."

"Hopefully, with someone by his side," Charles said in a comforting tone.

"Yes, in fact, there were two people there for him in his final hours, and both are here today," and Charlotte pointed in Elizabeth and Mary Paget's direction. "Mary was a VAD on the ward where Jeremy spent his last two days. After the war, Mary decided to become a nurse, and she made application for the program at London General Hospital and was assigned to me. After a few months, she had gathered enough clues from my stories to ask if I was a relation of Jeremy Lucas. It was of great comfort for me to know that my brother was so well cared for."

Charles nodded his head in sympathy. But this was too gloomy a subject for a man in love, and he excused himself, leaving Darcy to converse with Charlotte.

"Miss Lucas, you said there were two people who cared for your brother and that both were here. May I inquire as to the name of the other person?" Darcy asked.

"Elizabeth Bennet was the other person. Like Mary, she was a VAD at Le Touquet on that June night."

"But it was my understanding that she was assigned to the casino."

"Yes, under Sister McCrory, a tartar if there ever was one. She is currently my supervisor. Fortunately, Sister was able to get word to Elizabeth that Jeremy had been wounded, and she rushed to his side in Ward 18. I believe that is the correct number."

"I too was in hospital at Le Touquet in June, but with the flu."

"Oh yes, June 1918. It was in that month when the first wave of influenza hit. In fact, Elizabeth also caught the flu and was dreadfully ill and was sent home, but, miraculously, she fully recovered."

"But if I understand you correctly, your brother was at Le Touquet in June 1918 in Ward 18?"

"Yes, is that the ward you were on?"

"My memory is not as good as yours, Miss Lucas. I only know that I was at the same hospital at the same time as Miss Elizabeth."

* * *

Lizzy had observed William's conversation with Charlotte Lucas and was puzzled by his expression. It was almost as if her friend had shared something unpleasant with him, but knowing Charlotte, that did not seem likely. Because of her concern, Lizzy excused herself and walked in his direction. But there were so many familiar faces who had come to Meryton for the unveiling of the monument that she was waylaid time and time again, and she was unable to speak with William until they were in the car.

On the ride to Longbourn, William said little, but she attributed his quiet mood to the solemnity of the occasion. There were a dozen names on that memorial, a remarkable sacrifice for a village the size of Meryton, and she was afraid that the day might have dredged up painful memories of the war.

When they pulled into the drive, William turned to her and told her that they needed to talk, and any hope that this was the moment when he would ask her to be his wife was dispelled by the tone of his voice. She was about to ask him about his change in mood when Jane and Bingley tapped on the glass, and Darcy rolled down the window.

"Come in for a drink," Charles said. When Darcy showed no sign of moving, Charles told him that he had better come into the house, "that is, if you want to be my best man."

Lizzy and William followed the couple into the house so that they might join in the celebration of their engagement. With Mrs. Bennet overjoyed, Mr. Bennet pleased, Kitty smiling, and Lizzy elated, all the Bennets agreed that it was the perfect conclusion to a day with too many sad memories, and a bottle of champagne was called for and the servants encouraged to join in.

Darcy shook his friend's hand and congratulated him on finding such a beautiful, intelligent, and charming partner, causing Jane to blush and Lizzy to beam, and she wondered if she would ever hear such words spoken on her behalf. After an evening in which Darcy repeatedly embarrassed Charles with tales of their days at Cambridge and on holiday in

Europe in the glory days before the war, Lizzy walked with William to the car. But instead of kissing her goodnight, he whispered, "I know what happened at Le Touquet. You don't have to pretend anymore." He got into the car and drove away.

Chapter 14

Darcy couldn't remember when he had been angrier. All these months, Elizabeth had been playing him as a fool. Although she had appeared to be sympathetic to his misery, she had refused to provide the one piece of information that could possibly have proved to be a cure for all that he suffered and continued to suffer. And why had she done it? Because of some pre-war sensibility that he would consider her to be less than a lady because she had comforted him by lying by his side? For God's sakes, it was wartime. In the midst of so much death and destruction, there was no such thing as "normal." Did she really believe that he would judge her harshly for such a kind gesture?

Darcy was on his third whisky when Bingley came home. Because this was such an important day for his friend, he had a role to play, and Darcy would play it, despite the pain he was feeling after having been betrayed by the woman he loved.

"Well, here is the groom-to-be and one who knows how to keep a secret," Darcy said, raising his glass.

"Honestly, Darcy, I didn't know I would propose today. I don't even have a ring for Jane. Well, actually, I do, but it is in London. It belonged to my mother, and I am having it resized. Apparently, my mother had very fat fingers. But, today, with all the speeches and reminiscences, I felt myself sinking under the weight of it all, and as soon as I could, I pulled Jane aside and asked her to marry me."

"I am surprised you didn't do it sooner."

"I would have, believe me, but I wanted her to understand what she was getting into. It was only last week that I pulled off my boot and showed her where my foot had once been. You know, she is not like Elizabeth. She isn't used to seeing serrated flesh and torn limbs."

"And what was Jane's reaction?"

"All she said was 'Does it still hurt?' and then she kissed me and said no more. Darcy, honestly, I am the most fortunate of men, but a tired one, so I am going to go to bed." But he soon returned. "I almost forgot. Elizabeth gave me a love note for you," he said, winking at his friend, whom he believed would shortly be making an announcement of his own.

While Darcy opened the envelope, he believed that he would be reading words of contrition. Elizabeth would try to explain the inexplicable, but that was not what was written on the paper: *Yes, we* do *need to talk because I don't have a clue as to what you are talking about. Elizabeth*

Darcy felt a chill go down his spine. Those words were not penned by a woman who was experiencing remorse. Instead, they were written by a very angry lady, and all her anger was directed at him.

* * *

Before leaving for London, Darcy had sent Tim Smart with a message for Elizabeth, explaining that he had a doctor's appointment and that they would talk as soon as he returned. What he didn't say was that he was meeting with his psychiatrist and not his medical doctor.

On the train up to town, a calmer Darcy went over every minute of his time spent with Elizabeth, and after doing so, he realized that she was incapable of deception. But how was it possible that she could not remember the one time she had got into bed with a man. He had no doubt that she was a virgin, and not just in the matter of having carnal knowledge of a man, but in the matter of kisses and touches as well. He could tell by the way she had responded that these things were new to her experience. Was it the shame associated with having a man, who was not her husband or even her fiancée, touch, taste, and feel her body that had caused her to lock the whole of their time together away in some deep recess of her mind? He could only hope that Dr. Clarkson would have the answers.

Dr. Clarkson had asked Darcy to meet him at his office and not at the hospital where they had first met. The doctor was slowly increasing the hours he spent with his own private patients, and some of the sessions actually did not involve veterans of The Great War, a welcomed relief after years spent listening to the most horrific remembrances and watching men fall apart in front of him.

"Good to see you again, William," he said, gesturing to a leather chair in front of his desk. "You are looking well."

"I am well." With no preface, he asked the question that had been plaguing him. "Is it possible for someone to completely erase a memory from her mind?"

"Well, shall we begin at the beginning so that I might better answer your question?"

Darcy shared with Dr. Carlson the whole of his relationship with Elizabeth and then recreated all that he could remember of the night he had spent with her at Le Touquet: her kindness in responding to his call for water, her gentle touch, her tears over the loss of her friend and his attempt to comfort her, the moment when she had removed her pinafore and had laid down beside him, the exchange of kisses, and how he had awakened to find her gone, along with all evidence of her presence.

All of Darcy's inquiries regarding this beautiful woman had come to nothing, and the trail had gone cold when he had been transferred to a hospital that was reserved exclusively for flu patients. In the end, it would not have mattered if he had stayed at Le Touquet because Elizabeth had also contracted the flu, possibly from him, and had been sent home.

"So I ask you again, is it possible for someone to erase from her mind an event so personal, so intimate, so important?" Darcy said, the pain evident in his voice.

"Let us think for a minute about what we know about the young lady. She is the daughter of a country solicitor, brought up in a town where her social life consisted of a dance at the local assembly hall, Saturday night at the cinema, and church on Sunday. She probably had a flirtation or two with the local lads, nothing more. And then all that was familiar to her was blown away by the winds of war.

"After two years of endless bloodletting, with no end in sight, she felt that doing her bit required more than staying at home knitting socks and balaclavas for the troops, and she volunteered to become a VAD. Nothing in her experience would have prepared her for the servile work she would do on the wards. But that was nothing when compared to the horrors she would see once she was allowed to care for the patients. And the worst was yet to come as the men she would see in France would *not* be cleaned up with their wounds properly dressed. No, she would see men who looked more like pieces of meat than human beings, and all the while she was caring for these strangers, she would have news from home of friends being killed or maimed. But there was no time to deal with her own grief as there was too much to be done for those who might live if she provided them with the proper care. Darcy, by the time, Elizabeth met you, she was probably an expert at putting things out of her mind."

"I understand what you are saying," Darcy answered. "But on that night when her childhood friend died, we took comfort in each other. We were in a cocoon, safe from all that ugliness. Why would she not remember something that was good and sweet and pure? Yes, it was pure as she remains a virgin; I took nothing from her."

"You are not making enough allowance for her conservative middle-class background. This is not something Elizabeth would have done if the war had not come to her door. And there is another thing. You have told me that she came down with the flu; that you possibly gave it to her. If she was seriously ill, there could have been high fevers and/or delirium. The loss of memory may be attributed to her illness."

"That is possible," Darcy agreed. "It was just that being with Elizabeth was the most important moment of my life, and, yet, she remembers nothing of it."

"It is obvious to me that you love this girl very much. So my advice to you is to put Le Touquet behind you. That Elizabeth is gone, and you must go forward with the woman you met in Hertfordshire. Let it be new memories that bind you. Leave the past in the past."

Chapter 15

Darcy arrived at Longbourn with a bouquet of flowers, an opal cross from a London jeweler, and a new tennis racquet. He thought that at least one of these gifts would give Elizabeth pleasure, and it might improve his chances of earning her forgiveness for not seeking her out before his hasty departure for London. But what could he have said to her: "You spent the night in my arms in my hospital bed, and you don't remember that?"

Elizabeth thanked him for the flowers and cross, but toyed with the racquet in such a way that he understood her preference would have been to hit him with it.

"I would have written a love letter," Darcy said in a voice revealing his contrition, "but I was in such a hurry to return to you that I decided to forego that pleasure." Then he smiled, his most endearing feature, and she could feel the urge to read him the riot act waning.

"Are you prepared to explain your statement that I 'knew what happened at Le Touquet' and that 'I didn't have to pretend anymore'?"

"No. Because there is no explanation, and I am truly sorry for upsetting you. I would rather just forget it altogether."

"But I still have no idea of what you think I was playing at. From the very beginning of our acquaintance, I have been honest with you, possibly to the point of being rude."

Darcy pulled Elizabeth into his arms. "Not possibly, dear. You *were* rude." When she struggled against him because of his remark, he held her tighter and begged her forgiveness. "Please, let us put it behind us. The whole thing was stupid."

"And so it shall be forgotten." She slipped her hands around his waist and buried her head in his chest. "You frightened me," she whispered. "I thought you had stopped loving me."

"That will never happen. I can assure you of that." After nearly crushing her with his embrace, he kissed her with a tenderness that he thought had died in the war, and he felt as if he had finally come home.

"As much as I would like to stay here in your

arms and to be kissed by you," Lizzy said, "Charlotte is having a reception for the women under her charge who are shortly to become full-fledged nurses. You may come if you wish. Charles is. He is going to shoot pool with James Lucas while the ladies chat."

"I think I shall so that I might be nearby when your next urge to kiss me returns."

* * *

Since Jane was the only one of Charlotte's guests who had not served as a VAD during the war, she found little to contribute to the conversation, other than stating that with so many hospitals in France and Belgium how odd it was that two of the ladies present had both served at Le Touquet.

"And who is the other lady?" Mary Paget asked.

"My sister, Elizabeth Bennet," and she pointed to Lizzy who was standing behind her.

"Elizabeth Bennet?" she said, turning to Lizzy. "I thought your last name was Benton. We actually met at Le Touquet."

"Well, that *is* a coincidence," Lizzy said. "I must apologize because I do not remember you. Were you at the casino?"

"No, I was on Ward 18. I was the one who cared for Jeremy Lucas."

"How fortunate for Jeremy that you were there in his final hours."

"But so were you," Mary answered with great emphasis. "The orderly told me that you were with Lieutenant Lucas when he died. I should have been the one to hold his hand, but I was completely overwhelmed that night. Sister had come down with the flu and put me in charge of sending the less seriously wounded to a staging area for departure to England. Because of a rash of flu cases, we were quite overwhelmed."

"Yes, it is true that I was there, but my preference is to think of Jeremy serving aces on the tennis court and beating me badly, not lying in a hospital bed in France."

Nothing more was said about their service until Lizzy went to get a fresh cup of coffee, and she found that Mary Paget had followed her.

"I see that you have reconnected with Captain Darcy."

"Reconnected? I'm not sure what you mean. I was first introduced to *Mr.* Darcy this spring." Was there something in the air that had people speaking in some type of coded language? First, William, and now Miss Paget.

"No," Mary said, shaking her head. "You most

definitely knew Captain Darcy from Le Touquet." Seeing the confusion on her face, she added, "I was the one who found you with that gentleman behind the screen."

"Behind the screen with Captain Darcy? Whatever do you mean?" Lizzy asked and felt all of the color drain out of her face.

"On the night Jeremy Lucas died, you came into the ward while I was supervising the loading of patients into the ambulances," Mary whispered. "As I said, because of an outbreak of influenza, we were woefully understaffed. After we had finally got all the men into the ambulances, I went on my rounds, and that was when I found you asleep in Captain Darcy's arms."

Lizzy gasped aloud, and it was only because the other ladies were engaged in conversation that she was not heard.

"Please come with me out onto the terrace so that you might explain yourself," a frantic Lizzy said.

Lizzy feared that she was having one of William's panic attacks because her heart was racing, her palms were sweating, and there was a lump growing in her throat, making it difficult to swallow. But she must calm herself so that she might hear what Mary Paget had to say.

"Elizabeth, I have no desire to upset you, and maybe we should not say anything else as you seem to have forgotten the incident. Shall we agree to let sleeping dogs lie?" But Lizzy merely shook her head. She must know what she meant by her stunning statement. "Very well, then I shall tell you. After I saw you in bed with Captain Darcy, I made as much noise as I could without bringing the wrath of Sister Clayton down on me, and the ruckus *did* wake you. After I heard you go out the back door, I wanted to make sure that you had left nothing behind, but you did—your head covering with your name stitched on the inside. I sent an orderly around to return it to you. But with so many flu cases, I didn't have time to think about one VAD and one officer, and I put it out of my mind, just as you did, until tonight."

"I thought I dreamt it," a stunned Lizzy answered, and the tears ran down her cheeks. And the events of that night came at her in a tidal wave of memories, and the scene was so vivid, it was as if it had happened yesterday. She felt William's embrace, his touch, the smoothness of his back and the contour of his buttocks. He had opened the buttons on her uniform and had kissed her neck and shoulders, tasting her skin as if it contained some remedy for his affliction. But then he had stopped and had brought her head to his chest and ran his fingers through her hair, and she had fallen asleep in his arms.

"I didn't even know his name," Lizzy said when she could finally speak. "I didn't want to know it for fear that he would appear on a casualty list. I was leaving when he called out for water, and I brought it to him. And then he told me that he knew that my patient had died, and he placed his hand upon my hair, and it had been so long since anyone had touched me and…"

After handing Lizzy a handkerchief, Mary put her arm around her and told her that no one would ever know what she had seen that night. It was a secret she would take to her grave.

"Oh my God! William knows. That was what he was talking about when he told me that I should stop pretending. Somehow he learned that I was his angel of mercy—probably from his conversation with Charlotte. Dear God, what am I to do?"

Lizzy would have to decide quickly because William had walked through the terrace doors.

"There you are, Elizabeth. It seems as if everyone is getting ready to leave."

"Mr. Darcy, have you been introduced to Miss Paget?" Lizzy asked, while dabbing her eyes with Mary's handkerchief.

"Yes, Miss Lucas introduced us. Apparently, we are all alumni of Le Touquet." But neither lady responded to his comment. It was then that Darcy saw that Elizabeth had been crying.

"What is wrong? Are you unwell?" He looked to Mary for an answer.

"Elizabeth is fine. She just needs a minute." After squeezing Lizzy's hand, she said that she was going to rejoin her hostess.

Elizabeth refused to look at William, and it was in that moment that Darcy knew the reasons for her tears. Mary had said something about Le Touquet that had freed her memories from the far corner of her mind where they had lay hidden, and he took hold of her hand.

"I thought it was a dream—a beautiful dream," Lizzy said, unable to look at him. "I had arrived in France exactly one week before the start of the spring offensive, and with the first barrage, I found myself in a living hell with no means of escape. I was cleaning mud and muck out the wounds because I was too new to do anything else. And when I went outside, I saw the piles of limbs stacked like cordwood near the surgery, and I heard the screams, and I wanted to run away. Instead, I stayed, and in doing so, I lost my humanity. Every day, I arose and put one foot in front of the other, doing all that I was told and nothing more because my brain now functioned as a machine.

"And then Sister called me into her office to tell me that Jeremy Lucas had been wounded, and I ran. I ran as fast I could because I actually believed that if I reached him sooner rather than later that he would live. But, of course, he didn't. He had a stomach wound. Those were the worst. After he died, all I wanted to do was go into the night and keep walking until I reached England and my family. Not even the Channel was going to stop me from going home.

"And when you called out, I didn't want to answer. But the machine that I had become told me I must, so I got you a glass of water. But then you touched my cheek, and when you took me into your arms, I felt safe. And although it was but a brief respite, you made me human again."

After her confession, she finally had the courage to look at him. "William, I am so sorry. I truly did not remember. I wasn't pretending. I wasn't lying." She covered her face with hands and sobbed.

Darcy wrapped his arms around her, and after she had buried her head in his chest, she took comfort from his embrace and felt the same warmth that she had had on the night at Le Touquet. As he whispered "my darling" over and over, he held her until she was able to stop crying.

"So you have finally found your angel," Lizzy said, stepping away from William. "What must you think of me?"

"I shall tell you what I think of you. I think that you are beautiful, and I am referring to the beauty within. And I can now thank the person who saved my life." Lizzy shook her head, not understanding. "Your goodness and compassion restored my will to live. When I awoke the next morning, all I could think about was how I needed to live so that I might find you. And I looked for you and kept looking, the need to find my angel leading me on. But then I met Elizabeth Bennet and fell in love, and knowing that I no longer needed her, my angel flew away because I now had your love to protect me." He pulled her back into his arms and told her that he would never let her go.

"Elizabeth, I don't want to talk about Le Touquet anymore. I want to speak of a future with you as my wife. Because if you are by my side, I can face anything, not with an angel, but with you, my real flesh and blood soul mate. Will you marry me?"

Lizzy nodded her head, and after drying her tears, she told him, "I thought you would never ask me because of your...," but William put his finger to her lips, and she fell into his arms once again, convinced that her supernatural form had truly flown away.

* * *

After announcing their engagement, there was much to do and little time to do it in. Because it was a short two weeks before the start of Darcy's law studies, Elizabeth and Fitzwilliam exchanged their vows in a registrar's office in Meryton so that she could join him at Cambridge. During the Christmas holiday, when his parents and sister had returned from France, they would stand before the vicar at St. Michael's Church in Lambton near Pemberley and pledge their troth before God.

Following the ceremony, the happy couple and their witnesses returned to Longbourn where a celebratory dinner was hosted by Mr. and Mrs. Bennet. After the meal and all the toasts had been made, William and Elizabeth slipped away to a country inn on the London Road where the two became one.

"Before my parents arrive, we will go to Pemberley and make a long weekend of it, and we shall make love in every room in the house," Darcy said to his wife as she snuggled in his embrace.

"And how many rooms are there?" Lizzy asked in a voice feigning alarm.

"Since I intend to include in my count even the smallest broom closet, I am guessing that there are over one hundred."

"I shall be very tired."

"I shall reinvigorate you."

After they had made love once again, they continued to make plans about their future. But even with so many unknowns, in one thing they were certain: Their bond was so strong that nothing could ever break it because it had been forged in the fires of hell.

THE END

Other books by Mary Lydon Simonsen:

From Sourcebooks:
Searching for Pemberley
The Perfect Bride for Mr. Darcy
A Wife for Mr. Darcy
Mr. Darcy's Bite

From Quail Creek Publishing:
Novels:
Darcy Goes to War
Darcy on the Hudson
Becoming Elizabeth Darcy

Novellas:
For All the Wrong Reasons
Mr. Darcy's Angel of Mercy
A Walk in the Meadows at Rosings Park
Captain Wentworth: Home from the Sea
Mr. Darcy Bites Back (November 2012)

Short Story:
Darcy and Elizabeth: The Language of the Fan

Modern Novel:
The Second Date: Love Italian-American Style

Mystery:
Three's A Crowd, A Patrick Shea Mystery
A Killing in Kensington, A Patrick Shea Mystery

6268095R00083

Printed in Great Britain
by Amazon.co.uk, Ltd.,
Marston Gate.